Praise for *Medusa*

'Utterly transporting' – *Guardian* Books of the Year

'An impressive addition to the shelves of feminist
retellings, balancing rage with beautiful storytelling'
– *Irish Times*

'Immerse yourself in Jessie Burton's poetic,
powerful reclamation of Medusa's story'
– *Harper's Bazaar*

'A thought-provoking retelling' – *Daily Mail*

'A must-read for women of all ages'
– *Red* magazine

'Bracing and powerful' – *Guardian*

'Refreshes an ancient myth in a way that empowers
young women' – *Woman&Home*

MEDUSA

Books by Jessie Burton

The Confession
The House of Fortune
Medusa
The Miniaturist
The Muse
The Restless Girls

MEDUSA

JESSIE BURTON

BLOOMSBURY PUBLISHING
LONDON · OXFORD · NEW YORK · NEW DELHI · SYDNEY

BLOOMSBURY PUBLISHING
Bloomsbury Publishing Plc
50 Bedford Square, London WC1B 3DP, UK
29 Earlsfort Terrace, Dublin 2, Ireland

BLOOMSBURY, BLOOMSBURY PUBLISHING and the
Diana logo are trademarks of Bloomsbury Publishing Plc

First published in Great Britain 2021
This edition published 2023

A catalogue record for this book is available from the
British Library

ISBN: PB: 978-1-5266-6240-8; HB illustrated edition:
978-1-4088-8693-9; eBook: 978-1-5266-6239-2;
ePDF: 978-1-5266-6238-5

2 4 6 8 10 9 7 5 3 1

Printed and bound in Great Britain by CPI Group (UK) Ltd,
Croydon CR0 4YY

To find out more about our authors and books visit
www.bloomsbury.com and sign up for our newsletters

For my god-daughters, Florence and Elsa

Chapter One

If I told you that I'd killed a man with a glance, would you wait to hear the rest? The why, the how, what happened next? Or would you run from me, this mottled mirror, this body of unusual flesh? I know you. I know you won't leave, but let me start with this instead: a girl, on the edge, a cliff, her strange hair blowing backwards in the wind. A boy, down below, on his boat. Let them spill themselves out to each other, their story older than time itself. Let them reveal themselves until they reveal too much.

Let me start on my rocky island.

We'd been there four years, my older sisters and me, an eternal banishment we'd chosen for ourselves. And in almost all things, the place suited my needs perfectly, being deserted, beautiful, inhospitable. But forever is a long time and there were days when I thought I might go mad – that in fact, I already had.

Yes, we'd escaped, yes, we'd survived – but ours was a half-life, hiding in caves and shadows. My dog, Argentus, my sisters, me: my name sometimes whispered on the breeze.

Medusa, Medusa, Medusa – in repetition and decisions made, my life, my truths, my quieter days, the thoughts that formed, had fallen all away. And what was left? These jagged outcrops, an arrogant girl justly punished, a tale of snakes. Outrageous reality: I'd never known a change that wasn't monstrous. And here was another truth: I was lonely and I was angry, and rage and loneliness can end up tasting the same.

Four years stuck on an island is a long time to think about everything that's gone wrong in your life. The things people did to you that were out of your control. Four years alone like that sharpens the hunger for friendship and it bloats your dreams of love. So you stand on the top of a cliff, hiding yourself behind a rock. The wind slaps a sail, and the barking of a stranger's dog starts up. Then a boy appears, and you feel that your dreams might soon become reality. Except this time, life won't be outrageous. This time, it will be good and happy.

The first thing I saw of this boy – me on that cliff edge, peering down, him on the boat, unseeing – was his back. A lovely back. The way he dropped his anchor in my waters. Then, as he straightened up, the outline of his head. A perfect head! Turning round, his face tipped up towards my island. He looked, but he did not see.

I know a lot about beauty. Too much, in fact. But I'd never seen anything like him.

He was around my age, tall and in proportion although a little underweight, as if he'd been travelling far in that boat of his and hadn't known how to fish. The sunlight loved his head, making diamonds in the water to crown it. His chest was a drum on which the world beat a rhythm, and his mouth the music to dance above it.

To look at that boy was painful, yet I could not turn away. I wanted to eat him up like honey cake. It might have been desire, it might have been dread: I think it might have been both. I wanted him to see me, and was frightened that he might. My heart

3

astonished me like a new bruise that wanted pressing.

He seemed to be gauging the scale and insurmountability of my rocks. A dog, source of the bark that brought me to my lookout in the first place, dashed on the boat deck like a ball of light.

'Orado!' the boy called to this ball of light. 'For the love of Zeus, calm down!'

He sounded stressed, but his voice was clear. He had a strange accent, so I assumed he'd come from far away. Orado the dog sat down on his rump, and wagged his tail. My bruised heart lifted as I watched this creature. A friend for Argentus? I asked myself, thinking how lonely my dog had been for his own species.

But you know what I was really thinking: A friend for me.

Chapter Two

This young man pulled himself on to a rock, and sat with his legs dangling in the water, doing nothing except patting Orado on the head. His hunched pose gave me the impression that he didn't want to be here, and also that he was completely lost. He looked ready to jump back on to his deck, unfurl his sails and leave.

Do it, I urged him, silently, from my hideout. Leave this place. It'll be better for both of us. My cliffs are too high for a reason.

Just as these thoughts bloomed in my head like unwanted flowers, so too came another. Come, come up here. Come up and see me!

But he could never see me. Medusa, I said to myself. Imagine the moment. No way. For what would he see – a girl or a monster? Or both at the

5

same time? As if sensing my agitation, my head began to writhe. I reached up my hands and heard a gentle hiss.

Four years previously, I'd had lovely hair. No – I should say: four years previously, everything had been different, and the very least of it was that I'd had lovely hair. But seeing as I've been accused of vanity enough times by people who nevertheless thought it their right to ogle me, I might as well tell you: my hair was lovely. I wore it long and unbound, except when fishing with my sisters, because you don't want hair in your eyes when you're trying to catch a squid. It was dark brown, it waved down my back, and my sisters would scent it with thyme oil.

I'd never thought about it much. It was just my hair. But I would come to miss it.

These days – from the nape of my neck, over the crown and right up to my forehead – my skull's a home for snakes. That's right. Snakes. Not a single strand of human hair, but yellow snakes and red snakes, green and blue and black snakes, snakes with spots on and snakes with stripes. A snake the colour of coral. Another one of silver. Three or four of brilliant gold. I'm a woman whose head hisses: quite the

6

conversation starter, if there was anyone around to have a conversation.

No one in the world has a head like mine. At least, I don't think they do: I could be wrong. There could be women all over the world with snakes instead of hair. My sister Euryale thought they were a gift from the gods. While she had a point – it was literally the goddess Athena who did this to me – I begged to disagree. My creel of eels, my needy puppies; a head of fangs, excitable. Why would a young woman trying to get through her life want that?

When I breathed I felt the snakes breathing too, and when I tensed my muscles they rose to strike. Euryale said that they were intelligent because I was, varied in colour and disposition because I was. They were unwieldy because I was, and, at times, disciplined because I was. Yet we were not quite in symbiosis, because despite all that, I couldn't always predict how they would behave. Four years together and I was still not entirely their mistress. They scared me.

I closed my eyes and tried not to think about Athena and her awful warning before we fled our home: Woe betide any man fool enough to look upon you now! Athena hadn't hung around to explain herself further; shocked and sorrowful, we had fled soon after. I was still in the dark about what kind of woe she'd meant.

Anyway, it wasn't that I wanted anyone to look at me. I was so tired of being stared at my whole life, and now, with the snakes, the only thing I wanted to do was hide. They made me feel hideous, which I suspect was entirely Athena's intention.

I felt a twitch from the small serpent I'd called Echo. Echo was pink in colour, with emerald bands all up her body, and actually, she was sweet of nature. I turned in the direction that Echo was straining, and something snagged my eye. A tip of a sword, glinting on the deck of the boy's boat, under a sheet of goat-skin. Not just any old weather-beaten sword, covered in nicks and rust-coloured blood, like other men's. No. This was a brand-new number, and its point gleamed.

Never been used, I was sure.

Echo hissed, but I closed my mind to her warning. I'd been without company my own age for four long years, and the boy was so beautiful. I'd risk the sword if it meant I could keep looking.

*

It was Argentus and Orado who started it for us; our canine Cupids. My dog caught the scent of the boy's dog on the breeze, and before I could stop him, Argentus had rushed from our cave, making a long-legged skitter down the hairpin bends of the rock face towards the shore.

Orado, for his part, jumped off the promontory and loped towards my looming wolfhound like an emperor greeting his island ambassador. I hardly dared to breathe as our animals circled each other. The boy rose to his feet with a puzzled expression, looking up again at the sheer rock as if trying to work out how on earth Argentus had appeared. He turned back towards the deck of his boat, to where the sword lay partially exposed. To my relief, he left the weapon where it was.

'Hello, you,' I heard the boy say to Argentus.

At the sound of his voice, even up on the cliff edge, my snakes recoiled, curling into themselves so that my head was a nest of snail shells. Argentus began to growl. Hush, I told my snakes. Watch. The young man crouched to pat Argentus on the head, but Argentus backed away.

'Who are you?' I called down. I spoke in panic,

worried that Argentus's suspicion of this new arrival would drive him to his boat at any moment. And I spoke in hope: it felt of utmost importance that this boy should stay on my island – for a day, a week, a month. Maybe longer. A change in fortune was coming. I wasn't going to let it slip.

Startled, the boy looked up, but I knew he couldn't see me: I'd become an expert at hiding in plain sight.

'My name is Perseus!' he called back.

Perseus. Just like that, as if the clouds should know his name. No hiding.

Oh, gods. Perseus. Even now, his name sends a shiver snaking up my spine.

Maybe if Argentus hadn't snarled?

Maybe if I wasn't lonely?

Maybe if I hadn't spoken?

Maybe, maybe, maybe; why do we mortals always look back and imagine there was a simpler path? We think none of this would have happened. We think, for example, that Perseus would have sailed on his way, with his sword and Zeus knows what else underneath that goatskin, and I wouldn't be talking to you like this. I might still be waiting on that island, even today. I certainly wouldn't be here.

But it didn't happen like that. And the simpler path has never been for me.

Perseus began pacing back and forth beneath the scree that led directly to where I was hiding. 'Who are you?' he said.

Oh, nobody. Just a girl who took a one-way ticket to an island with her weird sisters and her dog. Nothing to look at here …

'Stay where you are,' I shouted, for he had begun to look for a space in the rocks to climb up.

Perseus stepped back and looked at the desolate promontory. 'What – here?'

'There a problem?' I sounded cockier than I felt.

'Who are you? I can't see you.' He made to move to where Argentus had emerged.

'You can't come up!' I cried.

'Do you have anything to eat?' he shouted back. 'I'm – I mean, my dog's quite hungry.'

'Sea's behind you. You could catch a fish.'

'Not my strong point.'

'Can't handle a rod?'

Perseus laughed, a sound to make cracks in my resolve, a sound even now to be found in my soul. So here was a boy who could laugh at himself. Rare.

'Please,' he said. 'I promise I won't bother you for long.'

'Where've you got to be?' I called down.

Perseus spun round, taking in the water's endless blue. 'Perhaps I'm here already,' he said. He spread his arms wide, turning back to the red of the rocks that towered to the sun. I wondered what would happen if I jumped off, tumbling down; whether he would catch me.

'All right,' he went on. 'I'll admit it. I'm lost.'

'He can't fish, and he can't read the stars,' I said. 'Anything he can do?'

Perseus ran a hand through his hair, and my heart weakened like yolk in a pan. Come here, a voice within me urged. Come close and let me see you.

And then, that other voice: Woe betide any man fool enough to look upon you now!

'I was sent on a mission,' Perseus said. 'The wind's blown me off course.'

'A mission?'

'I can't really talk about it. I certainly don't want

12

to shout about it up a rock.'

'Didn't your mother teach you not to speak to strangers?' I said.

'You could be anyone,' he replied.

'Exactly. You shouldn't be here, Mr Perseus.'

'I agree entirely,' he said. 'But when a king decides to ruin your life, you don't have much say in the matter.' Perseus kicked a rock and stubbed his toe, but kept his wincing silent.

What king was he talking about? And why had he clammed up when I mentioned his mother? I wanted to know. I wanted stories, company, closeness. But I was in an agony of self-doubt. Perseus should be left down there; I knew that. Argentus knew it. My snakes knew it. It would be better to ignore him, to tell him to get on his boat and go back to wherever he came from.

But when put together, the ache of loneliness and the bitter soup of boredom are more dangerous than any snake venom. And by the sounds of it, Perseus had powerful men interfering in his happiness. So: already we had something in common.

I looked out to the horizon. Nearly dusk. Stheno and Euryale, my sisters, would be back soon. What would Perseus say when he saw them looming from the sky – and what would they make of him? We could have a dead boy on our hands. I was going to have to make a decision, fast.

'I've just grilled a couple of fishes,' I said. (Epic words.) 'You can have some, if you like. There's a cove round to the left, with a concealed entrance. You can moor your boat in there.'

This was the most I'd ever said to a boy in my entire life, and when Perseus grinned, my heart began to sting. A matter of minutes and my life was changed. And, briefly, I will say it: happy.

Chapter Three

Of course, I didn't give Perseus the fish myself. I didn't want the snakes to scare him. Athena's voice never left my head. I placed his dinner by an arch-shaped rock at the entrance to our cave compound, but when I heard him approach with the two dogs, my words came tumbling out.

'You can't come in!' I cried. 'Stay on that side of the arch.'

'What?'

'There's the fish for you, and a cave about five minutes' walk, behind the big red boulder. You can stay there. If you want to, that is. I mean—'

'Don't you want me to come in?' said Perseus.

'You can't,' I said, avoiding his question. His presence was like an extra heartbeat in my blood.

'But why can't I?' he said.

15

I did not dare to speak: how to pluck a plausible explanation from the air?

'I'm … dangerous,' I said, holding Echo hard, for she was writhing like I'd dropped her in a pan of boiling water.

'Dangerous?' said Perseus, sounding doubtful. 'You don't sound dangerous.'

I looked up towards my snakes. Other than my sisters and Argentus, I'd never shown anyone my transformed head. The day Athena had transformed me, we'd run away forever from prying eyes.

'I think it's best you stay out there,' I said. 'My sisters are very … protective of me.'

'Why – are you made of gold and rubies?'

I didn't laugh. 'Because sometimes I do foolish things.'

'Don't we all?'

I squeezed my eyes tight and my snakes fizzed. 'I'm a liability.'

At this, Perseus laughed. 'If you say so. You live here with your sisters?'

'Yes.'

'Anyone else on this island?'

'Only us.'

16

'Where are your parents?'

'They're far away.'

'How far away?'

'You like asking questions, Perseus. Why not eat your fish?'

Perseus laughed again. It seemed like nothing I said could bother him. 'I'm sorry,' he said. 'I'm just trying to make your acquaintance.'

Despite a resistance deep inside me, I wanted to tell Perseus everything. I felt the risk in my blood, but maybe I was worrying too much? As long as he didn't see my snakes, surely it would be all right to tell him about my family?

'My parents are from Oceanus,' I said, my voice cracking with nerves. 'Hard on the edge of Night.'

'The edge of Night? Sounds amazing.'

'It is.'

'Then why have you ended up here?'

Oh, gods! How was I supposed to reply to that? His endless questions unleashed images through my mind. There was my little boat on the water, with a dark mass moving beneath. Next, a furious goddess, a flash of light, then a birth of snakes, my sisters struck with horror …

17

'Please, sit. Eat,' I said, my voice wobbling as I pushed the memories down. 'I know that you're hungry.'

The physical hunger inside Perseus overrode his thirst for knowledge. I heard him sit down by the fishes, unfolding the leaves in which I'd grilled them, and the aroma of herbs and fresh flesh was almost irresistible. To my dismay my snakes began unfurling with pleasure – for the fish or the boy I had no idea. Was this what attraction felt like – this loss of control?

'You haven't poisoned these fish, have you?' he said.

'Of course I haven't. Why would I do that?'

'Just checking,' he said, and I could hear the grin in his voice. I heard him start to eat. 'Oh, gods,' he said, chomping. 'Delicious. Thank you. Lucky me, washing up here. But there's two fish – why not join me? I promise I don't bite.'

Something else might, I thought, giving a warning tap to Artemis, a thin yellow snake with a particular predilection for grilled fish. Artemis was shimmying around, and so was my will, weakening to a sliver. All I wanted was to go out there and look at Perseus, just to take him in.

'So what's your name?' said Perseus, between mouthfuls. I was silent. 'Oh, come on,' he said. 'I told you mine. And my mother always says it's rude to take hospitality from a person without knowing their name.'

I crept out of my cave, a little nearer to the arch, listening to him eating my fish. No closer, no closer, I told myself. 'I'm Me—' I stopped. Who was I? Who could I be to this boy, that he wouldn't want to run a mile? Something in my blood told me to keep my name to myself. I plucked another out of the air and pinned it to myself like a painful brooch. 'My name is Merina,' I said.

'Merina,' he repeated. 'Unusual.'

I wasn't going to tell Perseus my name. I wasn't ready for that. And I wasn't going to let him see me. I was just going to sit on the other side of this entrance rock and pretend that boys like him washed up on my desert island all the time.

Chapter Four

Chapter Four

'So, Merina,' said Perseus. I'll admit how I shivered with pleasure at the sound of my new name. With a new name came possibilities, another chance at life. 'Tell me about the edge of Night. I want to hear about it. I'm so far from home myself.'

'On your mission?'

Perseus made a little grunting noise. 'Something like that.'

I didn't see the harm in describing my childhood home to him. My sisters never talked about it any more, probably because they were worried it would make me sadder than I already was. And even if they were just words, it felt comforting to go back.

'There was … so much water where I grew up,' I said, trying to find a beginning, trying to remember living on the edge of Night. 'Just one gulp of air and you were breathing sea salt. A place of streams and rivers and seas; water everywhere. Waves and waves of it, on towards the edge of Night.'

As I recalled the place of my birth, I could feel myself coming alive.

'Did you sail a lot?' asked Perseus.

'All the time. I miss it. I'd love to get back in a boat one day.'

'Well, I've got a boat. We could go for a sail round the coves.'

'I – It's … complicated.'

'Complicated? I thought you were a sailor.'

'I am,' I said, more defensive than I meant to be. 'Anyway, as I was saying: the edge of Night. Most people there wouldn't bob far from the shore, with their nets and spears for fish, watching the pass of an occasional ship, its sails bellied by the spice-filled wind. But not me.'

'You talk like a poet,' said Perseus. 'A sailor poet.'

'So let me tell you about the water,' I replied, my heart swelling. 'How it was wicked when it wanted to be. How it used to rise and fall, white and indigo on the heads of dolphins, and on those little mermaids who swam out with Poseidon—'

I stopped, my skin cold, my voice caught choking, my heart snapped shut. I hadn't uttered that sea-god's name out loud for four years, and in my very first conversation with a stranger, he'd caught me unawares. I felt the tears in my eyes, the bile in my throat, the quickening of my pulse, my palms damp, a sweaty dizziness threatening to bring me to my knees. Poseidon. His gliding bulk and fury. His power.

I closed my eyes. Come on, Medusa, I told myself. You're stronger than that. My snakes gathered round me in a halo of support, but I didn't feel strong.

'Merina?' said Perseus. 'Are you all right back there?'

I felt the clash of my two selves, new and old, burdened and carefree, hideous and beautiful. How was it possible to be all these things at once? I drew Argentus to my side and took a deep breath. 'Yes, yes,' I lied. 'All fine.'

As my pulse slowed back to normal, and I followed the undulating rhythms of my serpents, I registered a new sensation; a tingling, glittering thread of light from the base of my stomach, spiralling upwards into my throat. Could it be possible that Perseus … cared?

23

'The sun was shy on the edge of Night,' I continued. 'Here, it's like a burning punishment. Back then we were on moonland, starland, the patterns of our destiny spattering the sky. Perseus, have you ever seen true moonlight?'

'I can't honestly say.'

'Then you haven't. It holds a different brightness. When the crescent blooms to a coin, no lantern is ever needed, no fire in the hearth. The sand on the shore is a pewter ribbon. And up on the cliffs, hares live like silver trinkets, for the grass is smooth enough to line a jewel box. The air is cool. The sky fades bruise-blue to deep black shelter. And always the breeze, a hush for the troubled heart. A secret place. I remember it.'

Perseus was silent for a moment. 'I'd love to see it,' he said. 'And you were born there too?'

'Yes, not far from the cliffs and hares. My dad's a sea-god, and my mother a sea-goddess. They returned to the water, but my two older sisters – who live here with me – they stayed on land. They looked after me. Always.'

'So … you're immortal?'

'No, no. Nothing immortal about me! But my sisters are.'

I heard Perseus shift his position on the ground. 'Can you imagine what that must feel like – to know you'll live forever?' he said. 'Can you imagine being that different?'

I touched my snakes as they slumbered in peace. 'No,' I said. 'I can't.' I thanked some benign star that my serpents had not decided to writhe and hiss. I thought that maybe it was being near Perseus that calmed them, that they might see him as a friend.

'I'm like you,' Perseus said.

I laughed. 'How are you like me?'

'I was born containing the secret of my end. I'm mortal too.'

'Your life to come's a sum for which you do not know the answer,' I said.

'And nor should I, nor you,' he replied. 'For that is the right of every baby born, and man and woman after.'

His intelligence wreathed me like incense; our conversation was effortless. I inhaled it in deep and desperate gratitude. I closed my eyes and imagined Perseus reaching out to touch my face. When was the last time someone had spoken to me like this? Too long, too long. Maybe never.

Childhood: that country we all come from, but can never pin precisely on the map. Describing my old home to Perseus was bringing back the first fourteen years of my life. How I'd been so innocent, how I'd walk under the moon with my puppy Argentus, loping with his long legs by my side, frightening away the hares that quivered in the reeds. How I'd probably had idle dreams that one day I would marry a man like Perseus.

I'd been a friendly, thoughtful child, who tucked her hair behind her ears to comb the shore for starfish, five-fingered white bellies echoing her own hand in a greeting when she picked them. I would sing songs with my mother, who would rise up and greet me occasionally from the sea. I helped Stheno and Euryale tie their nets, and the three of us would travel deep into the channel between the edge of Night and the rest of Oceanus, to catch marlin and herring, the occasional octopus.

I was a sailor, Perseus was right. I would sit up in our little boat, while Stheno and Euryale plunged down into the water, dancing in the glow. And after the nets were full enough for three, I would row back and my sisters would swim to shore, and we'd grill a tentacle or two, seasoned with the thyme that grew in mad abundance on the cliffs.

It was a sweet life. It was my life. I demanded nothing from anyone, except to occupy my little space far on the edge of Night. A fishing trip, a joke around the fire, a song from my water mother, the body of Argentus to curl up with when time to sleep. A dream.

'And my dad's a god too,' said Perseus, snapping me out of a life long gone. The image of my happy boat speckled to nothingness. 'Yet another thing we have in common.'

'Really?' I said. 'Does he know you're here?'

'We don't have a close relationship. I mean, he's my dad, and everything, but it was my mother who brought me up.'

'Does she know you're here?'

Silence. Perseus cleared his throat. Was it distress, or anger, I could hear? It was ridiculous that we had to sit like this, either side of the entrance arch. But I had no choice. He'd take one look at my snakes and run a mile.

'She doesn't know where I am,' said Perseus. 'I … had to leave her. It's a long story.'

I thought of the king Perseus had mentioned, the one who'd ruined his life. Some sixth sense – or was it my snakes? – was telling me I shouldn't push it. 'Right,' I said. 'And ... have you come from very far?'

'Yes.' Perseus's voice was quiet. 'I don't know if I can ever go back.'

Yet another thing we have in common, I thought. Keep it together, Medusa. Maybe you have some shared experiences, but it's still better Perseus doesn't know why you're here. For how to explain, and where to begin?

He sounded so disconsolate, I had to think quickly how to cheer him up. 'Tell me about your childhood,' I said.

He laughed, and the sound weakened my bones. 'It was definitely weirder than yours,' he said.

'Who says?'

'I do. Listen, you might have a pair of immortal sisters, but—'

'Go on, then,' I said, feeling giddy. 'Prove it.'

'All right. My dad is ... Zeus,' he said.

'No.'

'Yes.'

28

'Zeus-Zeus? King of the gods?'

'The very same.'

'Wow.'

At least that explained the glowing aura that seemed to emanate from Perseus when he stood on the deck. Never mind being born with a silver spoon in his mouth; try a golden shovel. It was one thing we did not have in common. I grew up in happy obscurity under the moon, but Perseus had been drenched by the strongest beam of sun.

I laughed, the first time in four years. Oh the feel of it, the bubbles in my stomach, the fizzing sense of promise in my blood! I could have wept for joy. I still had it in me to laugh! Not many things since that moment have felt as sweet.

'You don't believe me?' said Perseus.

'Oh, I believe you,' I replied.

'My mother's called Danaë,' he went on. 'She'd like you.'

'How can you know?' I asked, grateful that Perseus couldn't see my blushing. Daphne, my particularly handsome serpent, with her black and gold markings, butted my forehead as if drilling me to take the compliment.

29

'Just a hunch,' said Perseus. 'Before I was born, her father locked her in a tower.'

'Why?'

'Because he'd been told a prophecy that any son born of his daughter would end up killing him.'

'And was it true?'

'I'm not a murderer, Merina,' he said harshly.

'Of course you're not,' I said. I cringed: how could I have offended him like that? 'I'm sorry.'

'It's OK. As far as I'm concerned, it's up to you whether or not to believe what other people predict for your future. People will always have their own motives. But my old grandpa soaked up every word. Became obsessed with this prophecy. It was so unfair. My mother's never forgiven him. She was a woman who'd done nothing wrong except exist.'

'Except exist,' I echoed in a whisper.

I closed my eyes, Argentus curled at my feet. I was lulled by the sweetness of Perseus's voice, by the aftermath of my own laughter, by the gulls mewling to each other, waiting for the last pickings of our fish. I badly wanted to know why Perseus had been on that boat of his – what was this mission he was on? What was it that had carried, or dragged him here?

'My grandfather was always terrified of losing importance, having his power taken away by someone younger,' Perseus continued. 'That prophecy made him dance to the tune of his own fear – that an unborn brat might strip him down like an old tree to use his bones for firewood. His solution was to lock my mother in a tower made of bronze, forbidding her to marry or to have any children, and vowing that he would never set her free.'

'I guess being old doesn't kill one's sense of the dramatic,' I said.

'Ha, certainly not. It only seems to make it worse.'

I imagined Danaë in her tower, one tiny window to let in the light. Her nose tipped to breathe the fresh air of the outside world, her ears pricked for daily noises that to her might now sound elegiac. A pair of stray dogs, rummaging through a pile of vegetable cuttings in the hope of a scrap of meat; a toddler's unbridled wail; the laughter of a group of friends, standing on a corner. I could taste Danaë's loneliness because it tasted exactly the same as mine.

'And then,' said Perseus, sounding pleased with himself, 'Zeus noticed her.'

Like Poseidon noticed me. I shuddered, pushing my mind away from such thoughts.

'He shone through her window like one of those sunbeams,' Perseus said. 'He surveyed her predicament. He told my mother that her life in that tower would be like living in a paradise, that the child they would have together would be the luckiest boy this side of Night. That child turned out to be me.'

'And are you?'

'Am I what?'

'The luckiest boy this side of Night?'

'Let's just say, in the last few hours I'm definitely feeling luckier,' Perseus said, a smile in his voice.

Echo, my coral-coloured little snake, woke up and shot straight as a dart in Perseus's direction. I peeled her slowly back in.

'So your mother ... agreed to Zeus's offer?' I said. 'Not everyone does.'

'She was tired of men and their promises,' said Perseus. 'And she thought about it for a long time. But yes, she agreed.'

I imagined Danaë, staring around the narrow space of her tower. 'At least Zeus asked,' I said. 'Which is ... unusual.'

'Well … you know,' said Perseus, sounding a little uncertain in the face of my weak enthusiasm. 'Anything was better than living out her days in a tower.'

I was silent.

'I wasn't there, Merina,' Perseus said, sounding prickly. 'It didn't happen to me.'

'It would never happen to you,' I said.

'What does that mean?'

'Nothing.'

'My mother wanted her life back,' he went on, his voice rising. 'She wanted her imagination reignited. All her options had been taken from her.'

'And so, like so many women before and since, she was forced into a corner and she made the time-less bargain?'

There was silence on the other side of the rock.

'What timeless bargain?' said Perseus.

'It doesn't matter.' I could never explain to this golden, glowing boy what it was like to have bad luck pile up at your feet again and again until you felt you were drowning in your own sorrow.

'You think I had it easy, don't you?' he said suddenly.

33

'Perseus.' I was desperate to reassure him.

'I was hidden, Merina. My existence was denied by everyone except my mother.'

'I know how that feels, I promise.'

'And then disaster struck, as disaster always does. My grandpa found out about me, because my mother kept asking the kitchen for extra portions of date cake and the cook got fed up with the constant demands. Grandpa investigated, and discovered a small baby in the tower. Me.'

'What happened?'

'He didn't kill us, for fear of angering Zeus. Instead he chucked us in a wooden chest and pushed us out to sea.'

'So both of us were babies who understood the water,' I said. 'Yet another thing we have in common.'

I was clinging to these commonalities, fearing how soon my snakes might wrench us apart.

'Right,' said Perseus. 'But we got caught in a huge storm. It was wild, Merina. Wild. Me, peering over the side of the chest, poor Mum in the middle of it trying to cling on to me, wondering how by Hades we were going to survive.'

'No doubt adding Zeus to her list of men to curse.'

'Exactly!' Perseus laughed.

It was better when we were telling the tale together. We were back on solid ground. I'd never, ever known such symphony.

'And how did you survive?' I asked.

'We got lucky. Poseidon saved us.'

A twitch on my snakes, a desire to scream, and just like that, my sense of safety shattered. The music we'd been making fizzled in the face of the one commonality I did not desire. To hear that god's name from Perseus's mouth made my stomach ache. My snakes rose up and began to hiss, fangs bared, writhing in fury. I edged away from the entrance arch so he couldn't hear them.

'What's going on back there?' Perseus said. 'Merina, are you all right? Shall I come in?'

I heard him rising to his feet. 'No!' I said. 'No!'

'Merina, please. Let me come in.'

'It's nothing.'

I grabbed all my snakes in one hand and squeezed their heads to shut them up. I understood their fury: it was the same as mine. 'Just my cauldron coming to the boil!' I shouted. 'Just some water splashed on to the rocks!'

'All right.' The hissing had stopped, but Perseus didn't sound convinced. 'But if you need any help—'

'Please,' I said, letting the snakes go limp and wiping the tears from my eyes, Poseidon's name slithering through my mind on a loop. 'Perseus, for both of us, just stay where you are.'

For now, he obeyed, but I could taste his confusion on the air. I wanted so much to tell him the truth, to show him these snakes, to tell him my story. But I didn't know how. We sat in silence either side of the rock – a silence more awkward and spiky, more painful even, than when my snakes were angry.

I closed my eyes. Poseidon, someone I hated so much, doing something loving for another soul? It was agony. Of all the gods to help Danaë, why did it have to be him? A mother and her child soon to die in a storm, bobbing around in a wooden chest. So Poseidon, bountiful god of the sea, rescues her. How kind of him.

But here's the thing: without Poseidon, there'd be no Perseus on my island. This truth was unavoidable. I could hardly bear its paradox. I pictured a familiar wall of water, my own little boat, Poseidon's looming, leering face, his shadow in Athena's temple. What happened after –

I shook my head – No, no, I would not let those memories win. But the more this boy was in my company, the more these broken moments came to me. Even though he was on the other side of the rock, I could feel his presence pulling my story out of me on a blood-coloured thread.

'It's inexplicable,' I said. 'To whom the gods are fair and foul.'

Perseus sighed. I stirred, smoothing down the scales of my snakes. It was fine, everything was fine. 'So what happened to you, Perseus, after Pos— after the sea was calmed?'

'A fisherman found us,' said Perseus. 'He pulled the wooden chest in from the water. Dry land! Mum says she clutched me to her chest and kissed the earth like a long-lost lover. We'd washed up in a place called Seriphos.'

'Seriphos?'

'Just a city. Markets, palaces. A few fields round the outside, and then the sea.'

'What sort of palaces?'

'Oh, you know. Palaces.'

37

I didn't know. Of course I didn't know. I lived in a cave. 'I haven't seen many palaces in my time,' I said.

'Well, it was better than bobbing around in a wooden chest, I'll say that.'

Perseus didn't seem to want to talk about the Seriphos chapter of his life very much, but I was determined to wheedle it out of him. Then I heard it: the beating of my sisters' wings.

'What's that noise?' he said.

'Listen to me, Perseus,' I said. 'A storm's coming. You need to go to your cave.'

'But—'

'Perseus. Do you trust me?'

'Yes,' he said, sounding almost surprised.

I hugged myself, my snakes undulating in rhythm with my happiness. 'Then go. And take Orado with you.'

Perseus concealed himself just in time. Within minutes, Stheno and Euryale hove into view from across the purpling sea, their wings magnificent against the dusk.

'Hello, darling,' Stheno said, landing neatly and

folding her wings between her shoulder blades. 'Brought you an octopus.'

She untangled its eight tentacles before laying it in a cool corner of the cave. When I didn't reply, she looked at me with concern. 'What's up?'

'Nothing's up. I'm fine.'

Euryale stalked towards me, hands on hips. She looked over at my snakes; Echo, in particular, appeared to be in a state of bliss. 'You seem different, Med,' my sister said. 'Changed.'

I rolled my eyes. 'I think I've been changed enough, don't you?'

'Takes a Gorgon to know it,' said Euryale.

'Don't use that word,' said Stheno, flashing a warning look at her.

'It's not a dirty word,' said Euryale. 'What's happened today?' she persisted.

'Oh, you two,' I said. 'I'm fine.'

My sisters were right, of course. I was changed, except this time, thankfully, it was a change you couldn't see.

I thought about Perseus up in the cave. Talking with him had been so easy. He was my secret. I'd never had a secret, least of all one I kept hidden from my sisters, who'd done everything in their power to protect me after life had gone wrong.

Actually, I didn't relish having a secret from my sisters. The fact of it was like a crack in the earth between us. A hairline crack, but a fissure all the same: Stheno and Euryale on one side, me alone on the other.

I pictured Perseus's sword, discarded on the deck, hiding in the shadows of the inlet. A son of Zeus, would he still be as warm once the sun had gone? There was still so much to discover and I might never know any of it. These few hours with him, even though we were sitting either side of a gigantic rock, had been like opening a book full of powerful words – words that I had never thought would be mine to hear, but which turned out to have been written just for me.

I knew it was not a book I was prepared to close.

I managed a passable impression of serenity over the octopus that night, my sisters and me sitting round the fire, with Argentus occasionally whimpering. He lifted his head every now and then in the direction of Perseus's hideout.

'What's wrong with that dog?' said Stheno.

'Old age,' I said. 'Thinks he's seeing ghosts.'

Love had been a ghost for so long. Until that day, I could have walked through it and not even noticed it was there. As my sisters slept by the dying fire, I closed my eyes and let the embers dance inside my lids. I thought of what it might mean to have a boy admire you, not for how you looked, but for who you were. For your thoughts and your deeds, your fears and your dreams. Was such a miracle to be my inheritance?

To know I was treasured, adored and celebrated; to be allowed, encouraged to shine, to feel perfect in the majestic mirror of someone else's gaze – could such a life ever be mine? Maybe Perseus was the one to tell me.

Please, I urged the gods – and one goddess in particular. You've done so much to punish me. Athena, please let me have this sliver of moon.

I waited. But Athena did not answer.

Chapter Five

That night, I dreamed of Athena, the goddess who had changed everything.

Even in my sleep, and even though what happened was four years ago, my body still recalled the pain she'd inflicted. Up it came, piercing the soles of my feet and calves, my backside, into my spine, a cyclone in my guts and lungs. Ice and fire, that was Athena, clutching my heart, shooting up my throat, back down my arms, freezing my mortal fingers.

Perhaps I tried to wake, but I was trapped in the nightmare. I could hear my sisters screaming, the uncomfortable sensation of power surging through my blood, wave after furious wave like molten metal. As a girl, I'd never felt this way – as if my feet could kick harder than a god's, as if my mouth would pour forth truths so blinding that no one who listened to me would ever be the same again.

And yet, I was monstrous. Was I monstrous? What was monstrous? Is what Athena did to me a punishment or a prize?

I couldn't have told you. The gods are mad at best.

Suddenly, and still in sleep: my head. Oh, my head – freezing cold, as if Athena had plunged me into the ocean's deepest waters. I didn't know how long it lasted – seconds, minutes, days? My eyes hard as diamonds, everything crystalline – but I kept blinking, hoping to see how I'd seen before. No use: I couldn't – I could never go back to how I was. Athena made sure of that.

Hissing, heard for the first time, like waters poured on hot stone. A heaviness on my scalp, dropping past my ears – cool, solid, coiling on my shoulders, over and over. My head feeling double its weight. I looked to my right. A snake's head, gazing at me as if waiting for my order, its body writhing from my scalp.

From my scalp.

Next to it, another snake – then more and more,

more and more – and I realised my hair was gone, and in its place was a crown of serpents, sinewy, strong, all colours of the rainbow.

The pain, as quickly as it had transfigured me, slithered away. My sisters stared in silence, and I returned their look of horror at the wings now sprouting from their backs.

For the first time in my life, I felt that I could really see. Stheno finally spoke, her voice haggard. 'What have you done to us?' she asked the goddess.

'Three girls, or three Gorgons?' replied Athena.

'Gorgons?' said Euryale. 'You've turned us into Gorgons?'

'Medusa,' the goddess continued. 'Listen well. Woe betide any man fool enough to look upon you now!'

'What do you mean?' I whispered, barely able to speak, but Athena saw no need to give me an answer.

I woke to the dying sound of her laugh. Just a dream, I told myself, my hands making their way to my head.

Ah. Not a dream. All true.

'Stheno? Eury?' I called. As my serpents roused

themselves, I lay on my back, letting them uncurl, and I wondered what Athena had really, truly meant about woe for a man foolish enough to look at me. Since the snakes, no man ever had. I'd never put her warning to the test – but I believed her all right. I believed that something terrible would happen to anyone who caught sight of me. Why else would she say it?

After Athena had turned us into Gorgons, my sisters and I had taken nothing with us from our village except Argentus, tucked inside Euryale's folded arm. Their new wings, courtesy of Athena, skimmed against the wind, and I remember my hand in Stheno's as she lifted me over land and water.

Stheno liked her wings, I could tell. She was graceful with them. My reality, however, was a nest of serpents writhing in excitement over my scalp. Stheno was too polite to indulge her pleasure in the face of my despair, but Euryale had had no such scruples, doing loops all through the dark till dawn.

I sat up, banishing these difficult memories. The cave was empty, save for the slumbering shape of Argentus; my sisters were already gone for the day, out over the seas. What else they did when not

46

gathering food, I didn't ask. Sometimes diving deep, probably, to gambol with the dolphins. But all those other hours? Part of me suspected it was better not to know. Gorgon-stuff. The making of a myth. They loved it, but I would have swapped it all for a head of normal hair.

Perseus had risen early. He was calling for me – 'Merina, Merina, are you there?' – from the other side of the entrance rock.

'Coming,' I called.

I wondered if he'd seen my sisters fly off on the hunt for food. As a son of Zeus, perhaps he wouldn't bat an eyelid at the fact that they could fly, but I couldn't be sure.

Perseus was playing an instrument that sounded like a flute. It was very melodious, and I wondered where he'd learned. He stopped and must have laid it down in the dirt, resting for a moment in the sun. Only one of his hands was visible to me from where I was standing. One hand, browned by the sun, resting in the gravel. Fine hairs, golden in the light. In seconds I could have grasped it, kissed it, felt the warmth of his flesh, those bones and knuckles more precious than a catch of pearls.

I almost did it. But I remembered.

'Good morning,' I said instead. Argentus loped to my side, taking the role of guard dog. Hearing Perseus spring to his feet, I shrank into the shadows.

'Can I come in?' he called back. No mention of my flying sisters.

'Not today,' I said.

How long could I keep him at bay like this? Since he'd arrived, I'd not been able to stop thinking about the moment Athena transformed my hair into snakes. The truth was, before he'd turned up I'd almost stopped considering them as anything strange, but now he was here, I had been made aware again of how my outside self appeared. I felt displaced from myself, as if my heart and soul had been moved off-centre.

I could tell my snakes didn't much like this mood of mine. Some of them were twitchy, jerky, others were strangely catatonic. Absent-mindedly I combed them where they'd knotted through the toss and turn of bad dreams and thoughts, Artemis and Echo twined like lovers lost in sleep.

'I just don't understand why I can't see you,' Perseus said. 'This is weird.'

'Neither do I,' I said to him, untwisting my serpents' bodies. How many gnomic answers could I give him, before I had to confess?

There was a pause, so long I could taste Perseus's disappointment inside it. 'Did you not sleep well?' he asked. 'You sound weary, Merina.'

Perseus was the first person I'd ever met who seemed able to understand me without seeing me. 'I'm … fine,' I said. 'Just a bad night's sleep.'

'I didn't sleep very well either,' he said. 'I think this island's haunted.'

'Haunted? By what?'

'I don't know. A witch?'

We laughed: to talk of witches in such sunshine – what a joke. Yes, I wanted to tell him. This island is haunted, but by something far more powerful than a witch: my story, my exile, the reason I am here. It was I who echoed in these rocks and pathways, inside the roofs of these caves. It was my memories that acted as signposts to draw Perseus in my direction, but what might happen when he reached his final destination?

'So,' said Perseus. 'How about we go down to the sea and look at the rock pools?'

'That would be lovely, but—'

'Or we could go for a swim? It's such a lovely day.'

A swim, a rock pool, the sun in the sky: the simplest ingredients for a happy day, and yet completely impossible. For the thousandth time, I cursed Athena. I cursed Poseidon, I cursed the neighbours back home by the edge of Night, all of whom had made my life such a misery that the only option had been to leave. Was I to spend the rest of my life hiding in a cave?

'I can't come,' I said, the familiar ache rising inside me, my snakes drooping on my shoulders like forlorn ropes. I stroked little Echo's head in an attempt to comfort her. Callisto, a bigger snake, deep magenta in colour and quite majestic when she wanted to be, wriggled in irritation at my mood. It's not my fault, I said to her silently. Blame Poseidon, blame Athena. But don't blame me.

Callisto hissed, as if to say, These days, you're big enough and ugly enough to ignore the caprices of a goddess.

That might be true, I hissed back. But inside, I'm still just me.

'Why can't you come?' said Perseus.

'I'm busy.'

'You're busy?'

'Cooking. Cleaning. That sort of thing.'

'Can't your sisters do that for the day?'

'They go and catch the food. I stay here.'

'But why? You can't stay in that cave all day.'

'I don't know how to explain this, Perseus. I've … never had to.'

'So try me. Your sisters bully you, is that it?'

'No, my sisters love me,' I replied, bristling. 'They've always loved me, even when I – when Athena—'

'Athena? What's Athena got to do with this?'

Oh, gods, I'd uttered Athena's name. The more I talked to Perseus, the more I kept revealing. And I wanted him to know. I wanted to tell someone who wasn't my sisters what it felt like to be me – to have been hated, so misunderstood – to not even understand herself. My whole life, no one had ever stopped to listen, to ask me a single question. They'd just looked at me, and thought they'd found their answer.

'Merina?'

'Like I said yesterday, Perseus: it's complicated.'

51

'Well, I'm not going anywhere until you come out of that cave.'

'I thought you had a mission?'

'Yes, but I want to know about you,' he said.

'You might not like what you hear.'

'Nobody's perfect.'

You're not kidding, I thought, looking up at Callisto and Daphne having a play fight. I considered my options. What could I tell Perseus, and what could I keep hidden? There were nuggets of the truth I could hand over to him – an offering in the hope that he might understand. And what, really, did I have to lose? I liked talking to him and he liked talking to me. He was young, and so was I, and he was lovely, and so had I been, once upon a time. Maybe, by spending time with him, I could feel lovely again.

My snakes, sensing this mental vacillation, began to undulate, as if they too were working out the best path to tread towards this glowing boy, so that he might like me, understand me, accept me for who I was.

'Merina,' Perseus said. 'How about this: if I tell you why I'm here, will you do the same?'

It's the hardest thing in the world to explain yourself, to tell your story clearly. We are all of us such complicated creatures, whether we have snakes for hair or not. Who we are, and why we are like that – I do not think there is a soul this side of Mount Olympus who can effortlessly explain the twists and turns their life has taken, why they might prefer a fig cake over a honey one, why they fell in love with that man rather than his friend, why they cry at night, or cry at beauty, or cry for no reason at all. But still. It's all we can do.

'I will tell you,' I heard myself saying. 'I promise.'

Perseus and I were demanding an enormous debt of each other – a mutual acceptance. The offering and receiving of such a thing is greater than the greatest kiss. We were tiptoeing on the edge of what some would call love, looking down into its precipice, wondering what it might be like to fall in.

Have you ever tasted sweet danger? It's one of the best and worst delicacies, all at once. Best, because nothing – and I repeat, nothing – in life will taste as heady and particular and deceptively right, and just for you. Worst, because once you've tasted it, anything that comes after it will only be dull.

'Perseus,' I said, my throat constricting. I needed to make him understand, but I could hardly breathe. 'I do want you to see me.'

'Good.'

'But you can't – because Athena – because I'm … disfigured.'

At this word, Daphne took umbrage and rose up. She had a point: it was fair to say that Daphne in her serpentine beauty was the opposite of disfigurement. I'm sorry, I whispered to her, silently. Daphne coiled into an indignant small ball, and Echo and Artemis wriggled with glee.

And so, with that word and with that warning, our exchange of truths began.

Chapter Six

'Disfigured?' said Perseus. There was no alarm in his voice, for which I was more grateful than I could have imagined. 'How?'

'Do you mean in what way am I disfigured, or how did it happen?'

'Both. I want to know it all.'

'OK. Have you ever felt that every step you take is the right one? Or that every word you speak is one note in a long song you're going to sing beautifully for the rest of your life?'

He laughed. 'I have to say no. But it sounds pretty nice.'

'When I was little, my sisters never asked me to be anything other than who I was. Myself. That's a great gift, Perseus. It's a really rare gift. If I could bottle up that confidence, that sense of belonging, and hand it out to every child I might meet, I would. But in the end, it was taken from me.'

'I'm sorry to hear that.'

'Well. It happens a lot. One day, you're fishing in the sea with joy and abandon, the next, something's watching you from beneath. Something huge. Something that will tear your life in two.'

'What do you mean?' said Perseus. 'What tore your life in two?'

From my side of the rock, my mind tumbled, desperately trying to find the best way to tell my story. 'I'm not saying that I was, or wasn't, beautiful,' I said.

'Beautiful?' echoed Perseus, and I heard the hope in his voice.

'I'm not getting trapped in that game any more.'

'I don't want to trap you—'

'I know my worth. It's not my job to count those coins.'

'Merina?'

My temper was rising and I tried to control it. 'But what I will tell you is this: when I was young, the only times I'd ever caught sight of my reflection was in the shoreline on a particularly moonlit day.

I'd notice my face, distorted by the ripples from a fishtail, or the trick of a breeze – and think so little of it. It was just my face, Perseus. A pair of eyes, a nose, a mouth, cheeks, a forehead – all of it framed by long, wavy hair. That's how it was.'

'You were pretty.'

I sighed. 'Some people thought so. Others not. When I was about eight, one day, Alekto, a woman in our village, said to my sister Stheno, right in front of me, "That one's a beauty. She's going to be a heartbreaker." Her husband agreed. But another woman, passing by, turned to look. "Oh no," she said. "She's nothing special." "What are you talking about?" said Alekto. "She's bewitching! Look at that lovely long hair." And so it started.'

'What started?'

'The debate over whether or not I was beautiful. They ended up having an actual fight over my appearance, as if it were the only thing about me that mattered. I remember touching my cheek, flinching as if my skin were hot stone. I was so worried over what I'd done, causing so much trouble. But Stheno said I hadn't done anything. I simply had a face. I felt I should apologise for something, but I didn't know what. As time went on, it felt as if other people were trying to enter my body and put their hands all over it, holding it up to the light in a way I never had. They carried on staring at me, dissecting me as if I were a moving sculpture they wanted to turn to stone.'

'Why did they do it?'

'So they could fit me into their own picture of the world. So that they could take me under control. I wanted to run up the cliffs and hide in the grass, but their opinions were lodged in my ears. And from then on, as I moved from being a girl to a young woman, I became two people. I was the one outside myself, looking on, and I was also the other, deeper self, mute within my body. It was impossible to keep them together as one person. I was beautiful, Perseus. But was I beautiful? What is beautiful? Was I born to break boys' hearts? I didn't want to break anything.'

'And did you – break boys' hearts?' asked Perseus, something akin to jealousy in his voice.

'No,' I said, a touch impatiently, for the boys' hearts weren't the point of this story; my own heart was. 'But I stopped going to the village. I avoided Alekto, all of them. I stopped walking along the shore in search of starfish, in case I peered into the sea and saw that I had changed – that in fact, half the village was right, and I wasn't beautiful. I watched myself like a hawk while feeling like a mouse.

'My sisters didn't know what to do – to tell me that of course I was beautiful only made me rely more on the villagers' opinions. Such assurance from my sisters provided me comfort for a short spell of time, but it also made me feel foolish for needing it in the first place. But then if they told me that it didn't matter whether I was beautiful or not, I would suspect that I was hideous. I'd handed myself over to the will of other people. I felt that I had to be beautiful in their eyes, otherwise I would no longer be myself. I had to keep this beauty whole, for the stars to stay in place.'

'Beautiful or disfigured, Merina, it shouldn't matter what other people think.'

'Easy words. I should have ground the villagers' opinions under my heel as dust. But haven't you ever worried about what you look like? Actually, don't answer that. Of course you haven't. You're Zeus's son. Of course you're handsome.'

'You sound like one of your villagers,' said Perseus.

59

This stung me. 'Well, I think it's easier being told you're a handsome boy than it is to be told you're a beautiful girl. When beauty's assigned you as a girl, it somehow becomes the essence of your being. It takes over everything else you might be. When you're a boy, it never dominates who you can be.'

'But if you didn't agree with all their scrutiny, why didn't you just ignore it?'

'I shouldn't have had to do anything! Even ignoring it was an effort, when I could have been doing something else more useful.' I sighed. 'Perseus, when you're a girl, people think your beauty is their possession. As if it's there for their pleasure, as if they've got something invested in it. They think you owe them for their admiration. Look at your mother and how Zeus behaved to her, breaking through her window. The effort to maintain your outward appearance in order to keep people happy, and the fear if you don't do it, are exhausting. You, on the other hand, can do what you like. You got on your boat and went sailing on a little trip, and no one stopped you. You could take that face of yours away and keep it for the dolphins, if you wanted. Not me. I wasn't allowed.'

'What makes you think I can do what I like?' His voice was hard and angry. 'What makes you think I wanted to get on my boat?'

'I—'

'I'm sorry for how your neighbours treated you, Merina. I truly am. People are fools. But you're not the only person who grew up not feeling true to who you were inside, surrounded by people deciding your fate for you.'

'You don't know the half of it,' I snapped.

We sat in frosty silence, but there was a kind of exhilaration mixed in with my anger. Finally, I was telling my story. Here we were, revealing ourselves to each other, even though we were not even sitting face to face. I felt fine threads of possibility connecting us, thickening, tightening their knots, drawing us together towards what I hoped would become an embrace – an embrace of two minds, at least, if not of two bodies.

'All right,' I said gently. 'So tell me. What happened to you?'

'You really want to know?' he said.

I could tell he was still sore. 'I really do,' I said.

'Well, I know what it's like to have people decide

things for you, that's for sure,' said Perseus. I heard him take a deep breath. 'Since I can remember,' he went on, 'I've lived in Seriphos, at the court of King Polydectes.' He uttered this man's name as one might mention a particularly virulent disease. 'Your island already feels more like home,' said Perseus. 'I feel freer here than I have in years.'

'But why?'

'You can have all the riches in the world and it still feels like a prison. The man who saved us after the storm took us to the court of Polydectes, and that's where I grew up. I kept my head down, bought food at the markets, played with Orado. Seriphos was a safe place for a child to live. My mother and I had no money, but she was so loving to me, and people were always generous. And yes, they were always telling me how handsome I was. Poor me.'

'You are handsome,' I said. 'At least, I imagine you are.' I felt myself blush and was grateful for the rock dividing us.

There was a silence, and then he spoke again. 'Merina?'

'Yes?'

'I think you're worried about me seeing this …
disfigurement of yours.'

'No one's seen me for a long time.'

'I'll wait.'

'What if I'm never ready?'

Perseus sighed. 'I feel like I can see you,' he said.

'And what do you see?'

'I see dark hair.'

Daphne hissed indignantly and I clamped her
jaw shut. 'Well, it was dark once,' I said.

'Once?'

'It's … a different colour now. Quite a few
colours, in fact.'

'Sounds lovely.'

'Lovely's not quite the word I'd use,' I said,
continuing to wrestle with Daphne.

'You shouldn't be so hard on yourself. I bet
you're quite … tall?'

'True.'

'And … you have green eyes?'

'Nope,' I said. 'Brown.'

'And I know you have a beautiful mouth.'

I said nothing to this, my skin tingling with pleasure and fear, but Perseus didn't stop. 'Just to see you

63

for a few seconds would be worth all those weeks I spent at sea—'

'I think you'd better get on with your story,' I said, finally releasing Daphne.

He laughed. 'All right. If you can believe it, by fifteen I was insufferable. I was the apple of everyone's eye.'

I thought about the villagers back home, how their admiration for me had turned to hate. 'You were told you were attractive, but no one punished you for it?' I said. 'Sounds terrible.'

'Life was all right,' he said. 'My mother and I were safe. I had a girlfriend.'

Callisto reared from my head, as if to strike in Perseus's direction. I held her down, hard, feeling her indignation pulsing in my palm. I tried to ignore her. Such indignation was ridiculous, whether it was in a mortal or a snake – Perseus was more than entitled to his life. 'A girlfriend?' I said.

'Her name was Driana.'

'Is she ... still your girlfriend?'

'When I left, she was. We fought about my leaving. She didn't want me to go, but I had to.'

'And now?'

64

'I don't know.'

'Why don't you know?' I heard him shift upon the gravel. 'Why were you talking about seeing my beautiful mouth, if you already had a girlfriend?'

'We weren't serious, Merina.'

'Right.'

'She's probably moved on. I've been gone so long.'

'How long exactly have you been away from Seriphos?'

'A few months. I had no choice. King Polydectes … It's a different life, Merina. Being here with you … I feel like a different me.'

'So do I,' I whispered under my breath.

'Driana's nice though,' Perseus added. 'You'd like her.'

Nice. I wondered if anyone would ever describe me as 'nice', and whether I'd even want them to. I tried to imagine a universe in which it might be possible that I would like Driana, but I'm afraid I was too petty to manage it. Driana had had Perseus's hand in hers, his mouth on hers! Days, drifting together – in olive groves, probably, under a gentle sun, not in baking heat like on my barren island. I pictured them taking an early dinner at some excellent Seriphosian establishment, whispering to each other over the candlelit table of bread, their gazes a connecting thread for them alone, sure in the security of each other's hearts.

I wanted it for myself. And even now, even after everything that had happened to me, I wanted to ask him one question: Is she pretty?

Ugh, she was probably as lovely as Aphrodite.

I despised myself. Come on, Medusa, don't ask such a stupid question. 'I'm sure we'd get on,' I said, my voice tight.

'About a year ago,' Perseus said, 'something changed.'

'Between you and Driana?'

'No. King Polydectes wanted my mother for his wife. But my mother wanted to be as far away from that creep as possible.'

As he spoke, Perseus's boyhood vanished from his voice like dawn vapour on the foothills.

I closed my eyes. So Danaë had double the rage then: escaping one king only to fall into the hands of another. I wanted to reach out across the ocean, to hold her hands and say, I know how that feels! Was it Danaë's anger that made Zeus and Polydectes 'notice' her? Was it her desire for the world outside, bursting from her heart? Was it her loneliness, was it her beauty?

I suspected that it was nothing Danaë did at all.

'My mother loathes Polydectes,' said Perseus. 'So do I. He's boring and rude but he thinks he's so interesting. He interrupts her any time she speaks. And he stinks. Why does he never use cologne?' He shouted this suddenly to the sky, as if it might have the answer.

I thought the lack of cologne was the least of Danaë's worries, but rage will work itself out in strange ways, so I said nothing.

'She tried to make light of it, said it was safer that way. Pretended it was a joke. Said we should throw peaches at him, then at least he'd smell better,' Perseus went on. 'But we never dared, of course. We never did. And as the weeks went by, his attentions grew worse. Polydectes cornered her at court all the time, for a "chat". You're poor, I'm rich, Polydectes would say. I'm a king. You know marrying me makes sense.'

'He sounds awful. And stupid.'

'He's a monster.'

'Right,' I said, wishing Perseus wouldn't use that word.

'Mum refused Polydectes's demands for marriage, but it didn't seem to make any difference. She was hounded, but it merely made Polydectes's desire for her stronger. He said she was playing hard to get. He said his desperation was her fault for ignoring him.'

'See?' I said. 'You can't just ignore these men. They don't like it when you ignore them.'

'I know,' said Perseus. 'She stopped going out, but he kept sending messengers. Then she lost her appetite. I didn't know what to do.'

I didn't need to imagine how Danaë had felt. Her own space, the little patch of land beneath her feet that belonged to her, invaded inch by inch by a man like Polydectes. I knew it too well.

'I tried to help,' Perseus said. 'But Mum didn't want me involved. She said it was her problem. But of course it was mine too.'

'Strictly speaking, Perseus, it was King Polydectes's problem.'

'True. But he wasn't going anywhere. So I told her I was going to solve it. Mum said she'd seen too well how the world worked, and she wanted me to hold on to the last of my childhood. She told me to keep out of it.'

'She sounds wonderful.'

'She is. I miss her.'

'Then you must go back and see her, Perseus.'

'Merina, I can't! That's the problem.' I could hear distress tightening Perseus's voice. 'I can't go back until I do this … thing.'

'What thing?'

'I'm getting to that. So: Polydectes was right about Mum having no money. We'd washed up in a wooden chest seventeen years ago, and still barely had a penny. Money would have been the only shield a woman in her circumstance could hope for. If she'd had money, she could have paid for a body-guard, or moved out of court. But we were broke.'

'So what did you do?'

'Eventually Mum accepted that she had another currency: me. She knew I wanted to help, and after a particularly, um … uncomfortable message from Polydectes, she got desperate. She agreed that I could speak to him.'

Perseus's voice thickened. I knew this wasn't

going to end well. 'And … did you speak to him?' I asked.

'Not immediately. I thought I had to look the part. So I started lifting weights.'

'Oh, Perseus.'

'Listen, Merina, you're not the only one who had to be one person in private, and another in a public show. My mother said that to deal with a brute, I would have to put on the mask of a brutish man. So I put on some muscles. And when I did, when I wandered around looking strong, it was like a world opened up to me. A world I didn't even know was there.'

'What do you mean?'

'Everyone almost expected me to behave like a strong man, like a hero already half written. They started to give way to me.'

'See, that's what I meant! Life's different when you're a man—'

'Yes, I know, but I stood in front of Mum like a bolted door. She hated it, I hated it. But my show carried weight, quite literally. I started to act the part. I was short with servants; no one minded. I boasted about all kinds of prowess, of violence;

everyone believed me, even respected me. I'd never been in battle, I'd never killed a man, but people thought I was telling the truth, everyone thought I was a force to be reckoned with. But I was just a boy made of smoke and mirrors. I danced with all the court ladies but I – I was ...'

'You ... ?'

'I was still a virgin.'

I thought of Driana. Maybe there weren't so many candlelit suppers by olive groves, after all. Inexplicably, this made me rather sad. 'There's nothing wrong with being a virgin,' I said.

'I know that, Merina,' he said. 'And that's not the point of my story.'

Touché.

'It was all a lie. I was a lie.' Perseus stopped. 'By Hades, I can't believe I'm telling you this. I've never, ever spoken about it before.'

'I'm glad you are,' I said. 'And I understand. When I'm with you, I feel like I ... like I can be nearer to who I really am.'

I wanted to jump round that rock and – and what then, Medusa? Woe betide ... I pinned myself against the rock instead, and closed my eyes, imagining

71

Perseus, a newly minted man, grinning through his mask at the Seriphosian ladies. 'So did it work?' I said. 'Did you get Polydectes to leave your mother alone?'

'In a way. The day of confrontation eventually came. Polydectes tried to push me to one side, but I told him that if he touched a hair on my mother's head, I'd kill him. I made a threat to a king that was punishable by death.'

'That's brave.'

'Or stupid. But the thing is, I'd do anything for my mum. And to my surprise the threat worked. Polydectes stepped away. He actually looked terrified. And I discovered the secret that my mother had already known. Polydectes would never accept her own refusals of herself, but he would when they were told him by a man. Even if that particular man still felt like a trembling boy.'

He fell silent. Above our heads, the gulls were coming in. We'd been talking for hours. The dusk was drawing in, the sky was lavender, and I felt so close to Perseus in that moment, sensing how hard it had been for him to tell this story. I felt so lucky to be his confessor.

72

'You'll have to stop for a while,' I said. 'I'm so sorry. My sisters.'

'But I haven't explained why I'm—'

'It's sunset, Perseus.'

'So?'

'My sisters will be coming.'

'Why are you so paranoid about your sisters? I still haven't told you why I had to leave Seriphos.'

'They've got wings,' I blurted.

We'd been in such a confessional mode – so close, so cosy! – that the words spilled out before I considered the consequences.

'Wings?' he said.

'Yep. My sisters have wings. They can … fly,' I added, unnecessarily.

Perseus laughed. 'Right. If you say so.'

'I'm serious. They can!'

'First they're immortal, now this. I knew this island was weird.'

'They might hurt you.'

'Why would they hurt me?'

'I did say you might not like this story.'

'Can you fly?' said Perseus.

I heard unease in his every word.

73

'No, no. No. I'm … normal. I told you.'

'That's a relief.'

'I … Look, just go, Perseus. Go to your cave. I promise I'll tell you more tomorrow. We made a promise, didn't we?'

'You're not going to … hurt me, are you?' he said. He sounded like a little boy.

'Of course not,' I said. 'Why ever would you think that?'

I like you, I wanted to say. I like you more than any human or god I've met in all my eighteen years.

'I'm sorry,' he said. 'I know you won't. It's just … I'm alone here.'

'You're not alone. You've got me. Just keep out of their way, and you'll be fine.'

'Why have they got wings?'

I thought about the moment with Athena, back on the edge of Night. The snakes spurting out of my head as my sisters cowered on the floor, turning into Gorgons. To answer Perseus's question would be to reveal more of myself than I ever had. I didn't know if I could do it. 'You're not alone, Perseus,' I said again. 'I'm here.'

I don't know why I did what I did next. It was so

74

foolish, to reach around the rock to take his hand. But I did, and it felt amazing. Perseus froze, but I held on tight, as if it were a piece of magic that might protect us both.

And perhaps he didn't know why he did what he did next – lifting my hand to his lips to kiss it, again and again. My fingers, my wrist, the soft inner skin of my lower arm. I closed my eyes and in my vision I saw his shadowy ship deck, the point of that sword. And I thought, What if my sisters come now? But they didn't, because for once the gods were kind. So we stood either side of that rock, our hands a beacon in our private darkness, opening the windows of our souls.

Chapter Seven

He's just a shadow at first, but he wants me to know he's there. I'm out in the boat by the edge of Night, Argentus at my side, my sisters underneath me in the water, winnowing the seaweed for pearls to string my hair.

It's him all right.

It's always him, huge as forty whales.

'Stheno? Euryale?' I call for my sisters, but all I hear is silence.

His shadow surges, the shape of him swells beneath my bobbing skiff.

Poseidon. Father of the sea, beneath the surface, watching.

Every last hair on Argentus's wiry back springs up in fear. He's rocking the boat, jumping from side to side as Poseidon glides, a threatening bulk of god, a terror in my bones. Dark stain in the water – what does he want? Why won't he go away?

Argentus tries to cover me, guarding my crouched body – but it isn't enough. When Poseidon wants something, it's never enough. The air turns still, as if Poseidon's put the day on hold.

'Look at me,' he says.

That awful, sea-blasted voice. The rasp of a shark fin up your spine, sucking the last breath of air.

But I will not look. I will not breathe his breath.

'Do you disobey, Medusa?' he booms.

He knows my name. How does he know my name? In my terror I've lost all reason. But of course: he's the father of the sea; there's no way a fourteen-year-old girl is going to outwit him.

'Medusa – last warning,' he says.

Still I refuse to look up. It's the only dominion I can claim. Some might say it's a mistake, but I don't care. Just because a god tells you to look at them, doesn't mean you have to.

A rushing sound, and I turn my head in the other direction. Oh, Hades. A huge wave hurling towards me – call it a tsunami, call it a wall of water, you can also call it certain death. Opposite, the other horror.

Poseidon, his chest a rock face, his belly like whale blubber, those blazing eyes, black oceans where not even a shark would dare to swim. I'm stuck between two nightmares.

'Do you want to die, Medusa?' the sea-god howls. 'Do you want your dog to die?'

'No!'

'Shall I stop the wave, Medusa?'

'Yes!'

'Then promise me anything I want.'

I turn once more to the tsunami: the sky has disappeared behind its might. How can the sky disappear? Anything's possible when a god's in a rage.

Water coming like a mountain. Fish everywhere, mermaids howling in pain as they tumble. Poseidon's power breaks their backs, their perfect fins sacrificed to his momentum. Argentus, scrabbling in the boat, desperate to jump and terrified to do so. We're going to die, I know it.

'I promise!' I scream above the babel.

'ANYTHING?' Poseidon screams back.

'ANYTHING!'

And just like that: the storm drops. I'm not dead. But all is silent.

What did I do wrong?

Nothing, Medusa, I want to tell my fourteen-year-old self. Look at me.

She doesn't want to look. She's scared.

Look at me: I'm not afraid to look at you! Listen to me. Medusa, are you listening?

'What did I do wrong?' I cried into the darkness of a cave, waking in a cold sweat, writhing and screaming on the floor. By my side, Stheno held my arm, shaking me awake. 'My darling, are you all right?' she was saying. 'Medusa, are you listening? A bad dream. You didn't do anything wrong. You did absolutely nothing wrong.'

'Where am I?' I said, just as I remembered – that I was not fourteen any more, I was eighteen. And that old life – Poseidon, the boat, the edge of Night – was a life long gone.

By the pale blue glow coming in through the cave mouth I knew it was nearly dawn.

'Him again?' my sister asked quietly.

'Him.'

'It's over now.'

Then why am I still dreaming about the promise I made? I wanted to ask her, but I didn't, because I

80

knew that Stheno would not have the answer. She held me tight as I wept into her side, my warmest sister who loved me like a mother.

You see, remembering's a blessing and a curse. You can't erase your bad memories, but a life without regrets is a life unlived. What you remember and how you remember: it makes you who you are. Maybe you have a choice about that, maybe you don't. But if I could wipe the vision of Poseidon, god of the sea, rising from the water, blocking the light of the stars, covering my skin with cold air, scrutiny and fear – then I absolutely would.

'We should stay with you today,' said Stheno, as the first rays of sun spanned over the horizon.

I thought of Perseus. I burned to be near him, even from the other side of a rock. I believed that being close to such a golden person would cocoon me in a greater warmth than the sun itself. How could I explain to my sisters that he was different? That he and I were friends, with all the things we had in common? I needed to find out why Perseus was here; I wanted to tell him why I was here. I felt sure our fates were intertwined.

'No need,' I said to my sister, putting brightness in my voice. 'I've got Argentus with me, and we need to eat.'

Euryale flew over to kneel at my side. 'Medusa,' she said. 'You mustn't let your dreams bother you. We know that it's hard sometimes, but—'

'Euryale, you have absolutely zero idea of what it's like. You think what happened to us is some kind of game.'

'Life is a game, Med,' Euryale replied. 'And you can play it.'

'Oh, can I?' I said. 'Well, I don't like the rules. In fact, it seems to me that there are no rules, because otherwise life would be fair.'

'You're unique, my darling,' said Euryale. 'The rules don't apply to you – or me and Stheno, for that matter. On this island we live how we want.'

Euryale might call me unique, but my heart was a victim of pain and longing as any other mortal's might be. 'You think what happened to me is something to be proud of,' I said, 'but it's horrible. How would you feel if you had a nest of crazy serpents on your head, where once you had a mortal plait?'

'Look,' said Euryale, beginning to lose her

patience. 'You're unlike any other woman in the world. You should enjoy it.'

'No. How would you like it – to have people frightened of you, to live in a prison cell in your own body?' My sister's look of ignorance enraged me further. 'Of course you don't give a flying squid,' I said. 'You're immortal. You don't even know what love is.'

'That's unfair, Medusa,' said Stheno.

'What's love got to do with all this?' Euryale said, narrowing her eyes.

'You think it's so great to be special,' I hissed, hiding my pain in anger, realising I'd gone too far, for we never talked about love on this island. I pointed at my head, my snakes stretched in all directions, baring fangs. 'It isn't. It's horrendous. I'm horrendous. I want to be NORMAL!'

My sisters covered their ears as my scream bounced around the walls of the cave. Echo, Callisto, Artemis, Daphne and all the other snakes flailed in painful panic. The very rocks that sheltered us were trembling, and Argentus fled.

'Athena chose you!' cried Euryale.

'Like Poseidon did?' I yelled.

83

'Forget that monster! Love's a fool's game. You'd do well to remember that,' Euryale said.

'Darling,' cried Stheno. 'You're not horrendous. You're our Medusa. You're as beautiful as the day you were born—'

'I never wanted beauty then, and I certainly can't have it now,' I snarled. 'Oh, just leave me alone. Both of you. Go. LEAVE!'

With their heads hanging – one in grief, the other in anger – my sisters walked from the cave. I heard their wings opening, their bodies rising – bodies which they loved as much as I hated mine. I envied them that confidence with such ferocity that my snakes turned to red-hot pokers spanning my skull. I was trapped; I was the one person I could never escape.

If only I could be Merina, the girl who cooked fish, the girl who boys wanted to stay and talk to. Merina, with normal hair. But no, I was Medusa. A monster. A hidden girl. All the things I never dreamed I'd be.

Perhaps the sound of roaring from my cave compound put Perseus off, for he was nowhere to be heard or seen.

Huh, I thought. Scared of a little roaring? But then, No. He's had a tough time of it. Give him a break.

And to be honest, I was a little scared myself. The rage my sister had released in me was almost over-powering. I feared Perseus would not come back again, now he knew a little more about my strange family. He'd arrived on this island and shaken things up, reminding me of everything I'd been through, everything I used to be and was no longer. If I was a locked box, Perseus might have been the one to find the key.

All this emotion, after some kisses on a hand! I know, I know. But consider: life hadn't been normal for me for a long while, and time on the island since Perseus's arrival had taken on a liquid quality. He and I were centenarians, and we were lambs. I hoped for love. I even believed that maybe it was being proffered, and I thought I had it near my reach. I could hardly wait to see him. I wanted so much to know why he'd washed up in our little cove, and I knew he wanted to tell me.

I tidied up the cave and decided to go for a walk to the other side of the island, to the hidden paths he would not know, where I might walk freely without being interrupted. I needed to put my thoughts in order.

As I left the entrance arch, I could hear Orado barking down below at the bottom of the cliffs. I crept to my lookout rock, and to my dismay I saw that Perseus was back on his deck. He's going to leave, I thought, and Callisto preened herself into prideful coils, as if to say she didn't care at all. But Perseus didn't seem to be setting sail. He was just sitting on a barrel, fiddling with a pair of sandals. He seemed annoyed.

'Orado, they don't even fit,' he was saying. 'Why did he give me these? Why can't I just wear my own?'

I wondered who Perseus was referring to. He didn't hurl the sandals he'd been trying on, but placed them down with deference, as if they were made of glass and might shatter. I saw how the sandals had wings: beautiful white feathers with pale pink tips, nothing like the storm-cloud colours of my sisters' appendages. They were fine as a dove's, yet plucked from a creature beyond my own imagination.

Daphne in particular peered down in curiosity, for she loved anything beautiful – but most of my other snakes began to writhe. They didn't like those sandals.

It's all right, I said to them. Look – Perseus doesn't like them either.

It was true, for Perseus was gladly pulling on a much-worn, battered pair of sandals instead. I liked them for their neat practicality, their style and subtle flair, just the same as their owner's. I liked too how Perseus talked to Orado as if expecting an answer.

I liked everything about Perseus, and my liking felt endless.

He pulled out the sword from underneath the goatskin, and finally I saw it in its full glory. It was enormous. It turned the deck gold in the sunlight – and it was far too heavy for him. The blade was straight and hard and true, so sharp it could only have been hammered by a god. Perseus could barely lift it. There was a ruby at the centre of the hilt, and from where I watched, it twinkled like a gleaming ball of blood.

I felt uneasy, looking at that sword. It was as if I were looking at something strangely familiar, but which only existed on the outskirts of my recent dreams. Perseus was ungainly with it; an unprepared but enthusiastic warrior. He laid it down, then pulled out a helmet, which he held as if it might explode in his hands. After placing the helmet on the deck, he reached again under the goatskin and dragged out a shining shield. He seemed to have an unending supply of weaponry.

I was mesmerised by this shield – as too, of course, was Daphne. This was even better than the sandals. She wanted it, I wanted it – all of us hiding behind the rock, snake or mortal, wanted it. The shield was smooth and round, as if the moon had fallen from the sky, as if Selene herself had descended to bless the waters round the boat. Next to the sword it seemed so pure, so bereft of bad intention.

Me and Perseus. Moon and sun, silver and gold. Why did he have this sword, this helmet, this shield – all these accoutrements of war with which to dress himself? He was surely too young to have them, as I was too young for what had happened to me; our bodies like precious metals that had been battered into weapons.

'Perseus!' I called, still hiding behind the rock. At the sound of my voice, he started like a guilty child caught raiding a toy box, surrounded by the evidence of his wrongdoing.

'Good morning, Merina,' he said, shoving all his spoils back under the goatskin.

'Are you going into battle?'

He laughed. 'I hope not.'

'Thank Zeus for that.'

'Are your sisters around?'

'Out hunting. They always leave early and don't come back till dusk.'

'Ah.' Even from up on the cliff, I could hear he was relieved. 'I was just going to go for a walk along the shore,' he said. 'Will you come?'

'Not now,' I replied. 'There's something I want to tell you.'

Chapter Eight

We sat either side of the entrance rock, our usual place, the red stone warm against our skin. It was only the third time we'd done this, but already it felt familiar, almost sitting back to back – if it weren't for the huge stone wedged between us.

We settled down as eagerly as children waiting for a present. The way Perseus had leaped up the path from his boat towards my cave had touched me deeply. Back in my village on the edge of Night, the people had turned on us. Was I crazy to be risking the same happening? Probably, but I had to take the risk. This island was so remote, I might never meet someone like Perseus again.

I closed my eyes, imagining him accepting what I had to tell him, putting his warm arms around me, his hands either side of my face, his mouth offering a kiss …

No, Medusa, I told myself. Remember what Athena said.

'You said you had something you wanted to tell me?' Perseus said from the other side of the rock.

'Yes, except … I don't know how to say it.'

'Is something wrong?'

'What do you know about … Poseidon?' I said. 'Other than the fact he saved you from the sea?'

'Nothing. He probably only did it as a favour to my father. After Mum and I washed up on the shore of Seriphos, I never saw him again.'

'I knew Poseidon too,' I said, trying to control my distress. 'When I was fourteen.'

'Was it Poseidon who disfigured you?'

'He noticed me, Perseus. The same way Zeus … noticed your mother.'

'Oh.' There was a pause. 'Right.'

'Yes. Except I didn't want to make a bargain. I liked my life as it was. I loved it, in fact. I was happy on the edge of Night. But Poseidon didn't care about that. He wouldn't leave me alone. He threatened me until I … promised.'

'Promised? Promised what?'

'That's just it,' I said sadly. 'I had no idea. I just said I'd promise him anything he wanted.'

'If you make a promise, you should probably be specific about it, Merina.'

'Perseus, he was threatening to murder me.'

'What?'

'He put a storm in the waters that would have drowned me if I hadn't made the promise.'

I closed my eyes, feeling the choppy waves inside me, seeing the sky darken again to steel, the stars disappearing as if a sulphurous cloak had been thrown upon their light. 'I said anything, to save myself and Argentus.'

'I see,' Perseus said quietly.

'He calmed the storm, but after that, he began to follow me every time I went fishing. At first my sisters said, Ignore him, he'll go away. But Poseidon didn't go away. Every time I went fishing, he was there. Every time. I was fourteen and I felt like ninety.'

'You should have stopped going fishing.'

'Why should I have stopped doing what I loved? Poseidon shouldn't have been there in the first place. He should have stopped following me!'

'But … yes. Yes,' said Perseus. 'All right. Yes, I see that.'

'There's something stubborn in me. I'm a half-finished map and I'm always trying to plot my points, and I won't have anyone do it for me. It was my boat, Perseus. My life. But up from the deep, there was Poseidon.' I shuddered. 'I would see his shadow rising, larger and larger, as it loomed towards my boat. He never broke the water's surface, but he was there all right. Hovering. Sometimes, when my back was turned, I felt a tug on my hair, and when I looked? Nothing. He'd forced me into this open-ended promise by threatening my death, but day by day he was taking my life anyway.'

'What did you do?'

'You'll be pleased to hear I stopped fishing,' I said. I heard Perseus sigh. 'Going out into the waters no longer made me happy. Argentus wouldn't even get in the boat any more, so I was bobbing alone up there while my sisters dived for fish.'

'Didn't he ever bother your sisters?'

'No. I was worried about them. While I was sitting there like a target in the little skiff, they were actually in the water with him. Euryale said they

94

were both big enough and immortal enough to look after themselves, but this was Poseidon – what might he do to them too? It was madness. The villagers had taken away my walks by the shore for being too vain and beautiful, and now Poseidon was stealing the last of my freedom. I didn't belong to myself any more. I belonged to Poseidon.'

'At least you were safe on land,' said Perseus.

I had to laugh. 'You don't think he gave up, do you?'

'Oh.'

'No. He started making storms again. Huge ones. The rivers burst, the fields flooded and the crops were destroyed. Then there was the lack of fish swimming shorewards from the ocean. The villagers began to get hungry, and Poseidon told them he'd stop it all if I would keep my "promise". She's snagged Poseidon, my neighbour Alekto said. Sitting out there, hanging over the side of her boat. Flaunting her curves all right, but won't give him what he wants. She made a promise, won't keep it – typical, fickle – and now we can't eat. She's taunting him.'

'But you weren't!'

'Of course I wasn't. I was just existing. Like your

mother was trying to exist with Polydectes bothering her the whole time. But Poseidon managed to make it all my fault. I'm not doing anything to him! I yelled at the villagers. I was so angry, Perseus. I'd never really experienced anger, but it grew inside me like a gift to myself. Stheno had always told me to be polite, but where had politeness got me? Making promises I didn't want to make or keep. We're all suffering because of you, said neighbour Leodes. I think she should go in the water, said Alekto. Let her go and land her big fish. Just give him what he wants, and he'll leave you alone, she added to me. It's how it goes, child, said Leodes. It's how to keep the peace.'

'But you didn't go in the water, did you?' said Perseus.

I leaned my head against the warm red rock and closed my eyes. 'One day, Perseus, as I was walking through the village, my legs gave way. I literally couldn't walk. I'd become so exposed, so sad, so desperate to press away the creeping conviction that I was doing something wrong, that my legs refused to work. The villagers made a crescent round me, but not one of them came to my help. My sisters were still out in the water, gathering their nets. I wanted to be free of feeling responsible for everybody's feelings, for the storms, for Poseidon. I didn't want to be a girl any more. I wanted to be a fish. I wanted to be caught and grilled by my sisters, then eaten to tiny bits inside their stomachs. Hidden forever, never to be me again. But despite the villagers' bullying, and Poseidon's pestering, no: I never went in the water.'

'You're very brave,' said Perseus.

I thought about this. 'I would have been just as brave a person even if I'd given in.'

We were silent for a while.

'There's ... more,' I said, scrunching up my eyes, willing the tears not to fall. 'The story isn't over. My sisters called to the goddess Athena to help me.'

'You've met Athena?' said Perseus.

'Yes,' I replied dully, touching my snakes.

'Me too,' he said.

'Oh?' I couldn't hide the hardness in my voice. 'When?'

'Quite recently. She was really nice to me,' he said. 'Very generous.'

'Lucky you. I got her on a bad day. She must have heard my sisters' pleas, because she turned up at our house one afternoon when Stheno and Euryale were out fishing and I was watching them from the cliffs. She said to me that I didn't look well, and I told her that she probably knew the reason for that. I begged her to help me get rid of Poseidon, because I'd tried everything and I didn't know what to do. And Athena said, Just because a god looks at you, you think you're special? Who exactly do you think you are? Everyone has problems.'

'That was helpful of her,' said Perseus.

'I got desperate. I told her I'd never sought Poseidon's attention, that I'd do anything to have him never look my way again. I said I'd tie my hair up, cut it off ...' I hesitated, my breath ragged.

'Are you all right?' said Perseus.

'I'm fine. I'm just remembering.'

'What happened next?'

'I remember Athena's expression changing. There was something sly in her eyes, a shining notion, a god's idea. You think your hair is beautiful? she said. I said I didn't think that at all, but I'd be happy to lose it if it meant no man or god would ever look at me again. I promised that I'd never seek a boyfriend, a husband, or a lover, if it meant Poseidon would let me go back into the waters in peace. I said I'd do anything. Athena asked me if I was sure about that. She said it was an awful lot for a mortal girl to promise.'

'She was right.'

'I wish I'd never said it. I wish I'd never made that promise.'

'Seems like you're always making promises to the gods.'

'Promises I never know the outcome of, until it's too late,' I said, scuffing a stray rock with my heel. Argentus whimpered. He knew where this was going. 'Athena told me to go to her temple. She said I was to let no one in. I should make offerings to her, and I'd be safe. I said I'd do it, and she disappeared.'

Closing my eyes again, I conjured that beautiful temple, just outside our village, amidst an olive grove. It had had its own neat garden of herbs and mountain flowers, with a fountain in the middle that sparkled in the moonlight.

'Under Athena's orders,' I continued, 'I made daily visits with Argentus – avoiding the sea, avoiding the village. I started to sleep there, Argentus at my feet. It became my shrunken world, but I didn't mind. Athena's temple was cool and comfortable:

low-slung stone benches and seats covered in soft cushions, a smell of amber and fresh bread, left daily by a baker as offerings to his favourite goddess.'

'That sounds good.'

'It wasn't bad. I ate the bread, leaving half for Athena, and sat on the steps outside, my back facing the sea, staring resolutely inland. Daily I offered fickle Athena my thanks. Daily I tended the olive trees. Daily I kept my head down. For a while, with all this avoidance, all this thanks and all this gardening, I did feel peaceful. I did feel safe. Poseidon couldn't get me.'

I fell silent. I remembered how convinced I became that my time in Athena's temple was going to be the end of it. By removing myself from Poseidon's surveillance, the pressure of his presence, by denying myself present love and future love, spending endless afternoons with Argentus in the tranquillity of Athena's temple, you might think I would have felt free.

You would be as naive as I was.

'Listen, Perseus,' I said. 'Take it from someone who knows. Sometimes, not even folding yourself into the smallest, littlest shape is enough. So you might as well stay the size you're supposed to be.'

'What happened, Merina?' Perseus whispered.

'He found me,' I said, my throat beginning to tighten. 'He came out of the water to hunt me down.'

'Oh, Hades.'

'A sea-god in an olive grove is a fish out of water, but he's no less powerful for it.' I swallowed, trying to keep a hold of myself. 'I remember seeing his shadow on the wall like a huge stain, moving under moonlight as the world slept. How he hurled Argentus to one side.'

'No,' said Perseus.

To hear his sympathy felt like my chest had been unlocked, and I was full of sobs that might never be quiet again. But I didn't want Perseus to hear my tears falling. I rubbed them hard, and Echo leaned down to gently lick the last of the damp away.

'Poseidon didn't care whose temple he was entering,' I said, my voice shaking. 'He just pulled the pillars down. I screamed for him to leave me alone, I called out to Athena, I said, No, no, no! But

101

in the rubble of that night, Poseidon took what I had never wanted to give him. Me.'

We sat in silence, the gulls wheeling loudly once again above our heads. In my mind's eye, I could see Athena's fountain, running with blood.

'Merina,' said Perseus quietly. 'Oh, gods. I am so sorry.'

I laughed without mirth. 'And afterwards, guess what? Some people in the village said I should be grateful for the attention. Not many gods deigned to give us mortals the time of day. But Poseidon didn't give me the time of day, for Hades' sake. He gave me nothing in return for what he took. He tried to make me lose myself.'

'Merina—'

'And the people who say these stupid things – perhaps they'd have liked to have spent half an hour in that desecrated temple, instead of me? I'll swap places. Gladly. But they never do, of course. They just want to tell you how much better they'd have handled it, how they'd have been able to say no.'

'You did say no!'

'So many times that the word lost its meaning. It certainly had no meaning for Poseidon.'

'How did you manage to get out?'

'He left, eventually. Somehow I crawled from the wreckage of the temple and found the road towards our home. My sisters had been roused by Argentus, and met me on the path. They took one look at me – dishevelled, dress torn, hair tangled, spirit missing – and held me in their arms, encircling me tight. I must have cried. Or did I? I remember so much – here, now, spilling myself out to you – but I must admit, I don't remember those moments immediately after.'

'Merina, I don't know what to say.'

'It's just nice you're listening. I remember the path, seeing my sisters, their arms round me. Argentus nuzzling my bare feet. Fleeing the temple without my sandals. That's all.'

There was silence again.

'It's a great honour that you told me this,' said Perseus. 'I won't forget it. No one's ever trusted me like you trust me. I wouldn't even have mentioned his name if I'd known.'

'It's fine,' I said. 'You didn't know.'

I leaned back against the rock, my heart now strangely settled. Talking to someone about my

103

experience in the temple, while never removing the sting, had somehow given it flight.

As we sat quietly afterwards, I could sense how my experience had moved a little away from me, how the revelation of my sadness had made me feel lighter – for how long, I did not know – but it was refreshing, amazing, to realise I could feel this way. I was in possession of my own story. I was the one who could either keep it or discard it.

I stroked my silently undulating snakes.

'Talking with you … Oh, by the gods, it's incredible,' Perseus said. 'You've lived such a life. It's not like being with Driana, or even my mother.'

'I don't like to hear that, Perseus. They'll have their stories too.'

'I know, I know. But listening to you … I've never felt like this.'

Was it the sound of my voice that he liked, or the words that I was saying? I ached to ask, but felt too shy. 'Like … what?' I said.

'Merina, have you … ever been in love?'

'Love?'

'Yes.'

'I don't know.' I hesitated. 'I don't think so.'

'Me neither.'

We were silent for a few moments.

'Perseus,' I said. 'You don't quite understand me. Not entirely. Not yet.'

'I understand that you and me are alike. We're survivors.'

'But that's just it. Despite the things we have in common, we're not alike.'

'Then opposites attract!' he said. I could hear him hesitate. 'I don't know if I've ever been happy,' he blurted out. 'I want to be happy.'

'And what will make you happy?'

'To see you, Merina.'

'You can't.'

'To be with you.'

'Impossible.'

'However you think you're disfigured, I don't care. Please.'

'Perseus, believe me. This can never be.'

'Oh, gods. Merina: I think I love you. I know it's mad, but I think I do.'

His words broke me open. Until I heard those words, I didn't know how much I'd been wanting them. They were only words, of course, and anyone can speak words. But in his mouth and in my ears they felt just right.

Panic shot through me, and my snakes began to writhe. What if Perseus decided to walk round the rock? What if this declaration meant that he'd had enough of my games, and would see me for who I truly was? How honest was he prepared for me to be?

I held my head in my hands, and my snakes fell forward like a morbid, warning, weeping willow. No matter, I said to them: I have to tell him how I feel.

'Perseus,' I whispered. 'I think I love you too.'

On the other side of the rock, Perseus sighed. It was a strange sigh, a sound of contentment, and one of sadness.

'I'll come back tomorrow,' he said. 'We promised to tell our stories to each other, and I keep my promises. You've told me about Poseidon. And I will never forget that. So tomorrow I will tell you why I left my home.'

Chapter Nine

Perseus returned to his cave and I to mine, promising to meet the next day, his love like a column of light I bathed in wherever I wandered. I could not believe my luck that he had found me on this remote island. I marvelled that we could fall for each other without meeting face to face, that the mortal mind was capable of such gymnastics when it wanted.

I believed the words he told me. I believed in the warmth I felt when I was near him. Until now, I'd never told a living soul the details of Poseidon. My sisters wanted me to blank it out, move on, start a fresh chapter. But you can't start a fresh chapter until you've ended the old one. Perseus had turned up out of the blue, the sunlight at his back, and my story had flowed.

Maybe there was something inside him that I

wanted for myself – the ease he had in his own body, his sense of freedom? Or maybe I'd sensed in him a slim chance to reclaim some of the happiness and magic the gods had taken from me? Tinder will not catch without a spark, and the fire was not all Perseus's doing. I'd been taught for so long to ignore what was in me – my own fire, my own voice wanting to be heard. And now it was time. I wanted to tell my story.

But as much as light lets you see clearly, it can also leave you with nowhere to hide. I was frightened by the force of my feelings for him, and where it could possibly lead.

I wondered what Perseus did during the few hours he was awake and not with me. He never wanted for food, for I left him a parcel every day outside the entrance arch. Maybe he walked the island paths? Or strayed from them – because despite his declaration of love, I sensed a restlessness. Not always obvious, but always there – at odds with his golden inheritance, his lovely dog, the bold way he'd arrived here on a boat.

I had the impression that Perseus usually did a good job of hiding his true self. But on this island, with no one but me to talk to, it was not so easy to conceal. And Perseus always wanted to unpack himself, like a delicious picnic I dearly wanted to eat. We were dealing in the market of ourselves now, presenting our parts, the swift and heady bartering of tales. Something bad had driven him to leave Seriphos, of that I was sure; but what were the parts of his story he wasn't telling?

I thought of the sword on his boat, the way it almost dwarfed him. The mesmerising shield, those winged sandals. But it wasn't those instruments of war that bothered me. Like fool's gold in lapis lazuli, something else was corrupting Perseus's confidence and I couldn't put my finger on what.

I pictured a possible future: Perseus and me, walking hand in hand along the shore, our dogs bounding ahead, the wind in our hair – or in my snakes – and everything whole and safe and fine. Or another future: maybe we'd take his boat and go travelling on the high seas? Or yet another: two small cribs, a homestead, sheep grazing on a hill, simple dinners under the stars. Another, another, another: these possibilities tortured me with their impossibility. Athena's curse still rang in my ear.

Woe betide any man fool enough to look upon you now! What woe? If she'd merely intended to damage my self-esteem, she'd managed it. But was it more?

In those weeks that followed, I didn't leave the house. I didn't even leave my bed. My sisters tried everything: sweet date cake, embraces, cool flannels, distance. The freshest octopus laced with lemon and thyme, grilled to perfection. But I couldn't look at an octopus tentacle without wanting to be sick. I wanted simply to hide. I'd been punished enough, just for being myself.

But Athena had turned up, of course. 'Where is she?' I remember her saying. 'Where is the little slut? Where's Medusa?'

At the sound of her voice, I crawled out of our house, blinking at the bright moon. I kept a shawl round myself, hugging it tight.

'How dare you!' the goddess said. 'You desecrated my sanctuary. Carrying on like that in my sacred place.'

I felt the floor sway beneath me. 'Carrying on?' I said. 'I – He ...'

(Back then, I couldn't say those particular words.)

'I trusted you,' said Athena.

Stheno emerged from the front door, rubbing the sleep out of her eyes, staring at our guest in astonishment. 'What's going on?'

By now Athena was glowing strangely, pointing her finger at me. It felt like an arrow piercing my skin: 'That girl destroyed my temple.'

'I rather think Poseidon did that,' said Stheno.

'And he would never have been there if it wasn't for her,' said Athena. 'You two are to blame as well, for letting Poseidon set eyes on her in the first place.'

'Oh, come on,' said Euryale, who had followed Stheno out of the house. I suppose being immortal, they had the guts to talk to Athena like this. They'd known each other a long time.

'Be reasonable, Athena,' said Euryale with a grimace. 'Be wise. You of all immortals should understand that Medusa had nothing to do with what happened in your temple. We could have put her on a desert island and he'd still have come to find her.'

'Nothing to do with it?' said Athena, pointing at me. 'She was a willing party.'

'A willing party?' I repeated, choking on my own breath.

'You knew what you were doing,' the goddess said to me. 'You promised him. And now my temple's gone, my fountain, my pillars, my groves—'

'I didn't promise him a thing!'

Athena sneered. 'Oh, I wouldn't be so sure. You fickle mortals! When you were out on the water, you made him a promise, girl, and what you allowed to happen in my temple—'

'Made him a promise? Allowed?' Euryale was shouting now. 'You think she set a candlelit dinner in your temple and sent that brute an invitation? And besides – any promise forced like that is more than allowed to be broken, and you know it, Athena. Poseidon intimidated her, he hurt her, and now he's trying to discredit her. And all Medusa did was utter some words in distress. She asked for your help, Athena. You said you'd protect her. So go and bother Poseidon about this, not her, or by Zeus, I'll—'

'What? What will you do?' Athena laughed; Euryale could only glower.

We all knew why Athena was laughing. She was one of the most powerful goddesses in the world, unintimidated by Euryale's threats.

Yet again I fell mute in the face of other people's

words as they discussed me. As the argument between Athena and my sisters raged, I stared deep into my spirit. Had I been doing anything to provoke him, either out in the boat, or inside the temple? Of course I hadn't. I hated the way things like this made you even more unsure of yourself. It felt strange to listen to a goddess being wrong, but I didn't dare disagree with her, for fear of what she'd do.

'Athena, this isn't really about your temple, is it?' Stheno interjected. 'You couldn't care less about those bricks.'

'It's about propriety and decency. Respect,' said the goddess.

'And not Medusa's happiness, or her right to walk about inside her body without any fear? No. The truth is, Athena, you're jealous.'

'Jealous?' hooted Athena, so loudly it would have been comical coming from anyone else but her. The goddess's eyes narrowed, and her face began to turn bright with a deep inner fury. I willed my sister to shut up as Athena pointed at me yet again. 'Jealous of her?'

'I see it clearly enough,' said Stheno. 'Medusa's more beautiful than you—'

'Oh, please …'

'– and you can't stand it.'

Stheno shouldn't have said that. She really shouldn't have said that. The truth is – and I should know, I've suffered both – that words can wound you deeper than a sword cut.

And so it proved.

On hearing these words, the hot burn in Athena's face turned cold. Her skin was almost blanched. She was staring at me with the most spine-chilling look of intent I've ever seen on god or mortal, before or since. The hairs on the back of my neck began to rise. I knew something bad was coming straight in my direction.

Is it possible, I wondered, that even goddesses let this sort of comment bother them?

Apparently they do. Apparently goddesses are just like me and you.

Athena's gaze seared my skin, her fury covered me like a shroud. As her power entered me, the moon on the edge of Night and the moonlight in my soul were eclipsed by the size of her rage. These were the last moments of our lives when my sisters and I could consider ourselves anywhere near normal.

*

I falter in my recollection here – for this was where my story broke apart, a whale skeleton left to rot upon the shore. How could I ever explain to Perseus what happened in my final meeting with Athena? How could I explain these snakes on my head, or tell him that I was a girl who was also a Gorgon?

I shook my head at the memory, and my snakes stirred. Echo and Callisto untwined themselves and bobbed around in the air. I realised a strange thing: I complained about them all the time, I resented them, and when it came to Perseus I thought they were a massive liability – but I knew I would miss them if they were taken away. They were part of me now; there was no going back. For a long time after Athena transformed me, I had hoped that Echo, Callisto, Daphne, Artemis and the others were just a temporary whim of a goddess; that I could return to how I looked before. But it never happened. Nothing I could beg or promise would take me back.

Artemis snapped lazily at a passing fly. And would you want to go back now, I wondered to myself, despite it all?

Yes, I missed the starlight at the edge of Night,

but what was there for me except a reputation unfairly in tatters, hated as a beauty and probably even more so as a hag, and a bunch of neighbours unwilling to change their minds about me? At least here I had some freedom to roam, to be myself, without the pokes and prods and commentary from strangers and acquaintances alike.

Euryale was right: I could breathe on this island. On this island we lived as we pleased. No one called me a monster, and no one attacked me for being too pretty. I'd come to love the rocks, changing colour as the sun moved – pale orange, almost-scarlet, powder of vermilion to the touch. Yes, they were jagged, but their sides were smooth. I loved to lie on them and watch their shifting shades.

I'd told Perseus that I was hiding, but maybe I wasn't at all. Maybe I had found my space to simply be.

Maybe I hadn't realised it, but I'd found a kind of peace.

And now he'd said he loved me. Maybe certain impossibilities were not so impossible, after all.

Chapter Ten

That night, I dreamed of another woman. It was Driana, stalking the passageways of my mind – or at least, a girl I thought of as Driana, for I'd never asked Perseus what she looked like. She was dressed as a bride, standing quite alone on the edge of a cliff, holding a bouquet of thyme and octopus tentacles. Her dark hair, dark as mine had once been, encircled her head with a neat coil. She was pacing, waiting for someone. There was a roaring rush of wind and her veil whipped off, turning itself into a ship's sail, attached to a boat that moved far off into the horizon.

I followed the boat in my mind's eye, and when I turned back towards the land, Driana and her bouquet had gone.

*

I woke to see Stheno sitting alone by the mouth of our cave. Her legs were crossed, her wings half extended, billowing gently in the breeze. She was very upright. If Euryale was the doer of that duo, Stheno was its thinker. Such a silhouette against the light of the sun! – the shape of which I'd doubt you'd see in Seriphos. She was so still I could have mistaken her for a statue.

Since the day I was born, Stheno had loved and protected me with a tenderness to match Euryale's ferocity. Euryale was strong and proud of herself, but I always felt that Stheno somehow better understood my fears of being different. I knew that what I'd said to my sisters in anger – that they didn't know what love was – was unfair. Looking at Stheno, her head now bowed, I felt terrible. For when Stheno had been looking after me, who had been looking after Stheno?

'Are you all right?' I asked.

My sister turned to me, the folds of her ragged dress fanning out upon the cave floor, her face drawn and pale. 'Good morning,' she said with a shy smile. 'Another bad dream? You didn't stop tossing and turning.'

118

'Where's Eury?'

'Out.'

'Out where?'

'Just … flying.'

Her evasion, so unusual, gave me a prickle of fear, loosening my stomach.

'Come here,' Stheno said gently, and I obeyed as if I were four years old, half of my mind on her, the other half outside the cave wondering where Euryale had got to. Stheno gestured for me to sit. 'My darling,' she said. 'Are you well?'

'I'm fine.'

'I don't know if that's true.' She held up one hand as I made to protest. 'I know that life has not always been easy for you, Medusa. There must be things that you miss. Things you worry you might never have.'

'I don't miss anything,' I said, crossing my legs beside her, feeling the heat from the ground even this early in the day.

My sister looked away. 'You've seemed absent at our dinners,' she said quietly. 'And then there was the dream of … Poseidon.'

'Stheno, it was just a dream. Just emptying my head out at the end of the day.'

119

'But why is he in your head again in the first place? You know it's never just a dream. It means something.'

I thought of Driana, standing on the cliff, her veil flying out towards the sea. 'Dreams are just dreams,' I said. 'They don't mean anything.'

Stheno frowned. 'Sometimes I think we should never have come here. We should have stayed on the edge of Night. At least there was life back home. Other girls …' She hesitated. 'And boys.'

'They didn't like me much before Athena transformed me, and they certainly wouldn't have liked me after.'

'You don't know that.'

'We did live in the same village, didn't we?' I said, and Stheno laughed sadly. 'There's life enough here, sister,' I went on. 'Trust me.'

'But it's different for me and Eury,' she said. 'We have … all of life – and you have one life.' She gestured outwards with one arm and I heard the dry rustling of her feathers. 'And you're spending it here.'

'You did what you had to do. We all did.'

Suddenly Stheno got to her knees and placed her hands either side of my face. She stared into my

120

eyes. It was a long time since we had truly looked at each other, and I remembered how her irises were much bluer than Euryale's, and flecked with sea green and gold. I could have dived into Stheno's eyes and felt safe forever, but I had learned the hard way that not even Stheno could protect me entirely. It was a truth that both paralysed me and set me free.

'Promise me, Medusa,' Stheno said, as if she had read my mind. 'Promise you're not doing anything that might put you in danger?'

'I would never do that,' I said. I held my sister's solemn gaze. 'I'm happy here. Truly.'

'Medusa, is there something you're not telling me?'

My stomach turned over. 'Why would you think that?'

'Why are you happy here?' she said. 'What, on this barren island, could possibly make you happy?'

'Being with you. Being with Euryale.'

She gave me a doubtful look. 'Euryale was right. You are different these last few days.'

'I'm fine.'

'Medusa, if there ever were someone, a boy, for example—'

'Why would there ever be a boy?'

'If there ever were, you must never deny who you are, or pretend to be the woman you think he would want you to be. You'll be walking on a lonely road that leads to nowhere.' I stared at her. 'If he truly likes you, Med,' Stheno went on, a little breathlessly, running a handful of gravel through her fingers as she warmed to her subject, 'he will take you for who you are, and consider himself lucky to know you.'

'I'll bear that in mind.'

Stheno threw down the gravel and batted her wings. 'Oh, what's the use tiptoeing! Medusa, I know.'

'Know what?'

'I do have eyes, Med. We're not in Athens, we're on a desert island. A small desert island.'

'So?'

'So if a boat moors in the cove, I'm going to see it. And I'm going to wonder who sailed in on it. And I'm going to go exploring.'

I couldn't speak. Visions of Euryale tying Perseus up for trespassing, or throwing him back on his boat, never to see him again, passed through my sight …

'And I'm going to notice the changes in my sister,'

Stheno went on, interrupting the catastrophes blinking like fireflies across my vision. 'Her dreams, her secret smile. The fact she's fallen in love.'

We sat in silence. The relief of telling the truth, of sharing this reality, was too tempting. 'I'm sorry, Stheno,' I whispered. 'I didn't mean to. I didn't invite him—'

'I'm not angry, my darling,' Stheno said. 'Don't you dare apologise! You've done enough of that.'

I could feel tears rising to my eyes. My sister's heart was bigger than Mount Olympus. She reached for me and put her arm around my shoulder. 'I'm right, though, aren't I?' she said.

'You are.'

'Who is he?'

'He's Perseus.'

'Well, that's his name, but who is he?'

I realised then that there was not much I could tell. Of course I felt I knew Perseus. I'd made him a mix of a real boy and the fantasies I couldn't resist building in my mind, as if I were a god, and my life a celestial canvas. But the truth was, when faced with a question like that, I simply did not know that much about him.

It was not a pleasant realisation. The small world that Perseus and I had been constructing together now seemed made of gossamer in the face of an outsider's scrutiny, even an outsider as gracious as my sister.

'Does Euryale know about him?' I asked, unable to hide the panic in my voice.

'No. Don't worry. I saw his boat, and then I saw him as I was flying back one day. Euryale didn't see him. You were very fortunate. I pushed the boat further into the cove. She won't know.'

'Please, I beg you, Stheno, please don't tell her. She won't like it.'

'I know she won't like it,' Stheno said. 'But what's this Perseus doing here?'

'He's … travelling. Seeing the world a bit. You know.'

'I see. Lucky him.' Stheno sighed. 'So he just … came here by accident?'

'He was lost.'

'Right.' My sister gave me a hard look. 'He doesn't know about you, does he? You've been hiding it?' Her eyes flicked to the top of my head.

'Well, I didn't think it was the best opening line:

124

Hi, I'm in voluntary exile – oh, and I also have a head of snakes.'

But Stheno wasn't laughing. 'But do you like him? I mean, really like him?'

'Yes, I think I do.'

'And does he like you?'

'I think so. What he knows about me, at least.'

Stheno looked away, towards the invisible horizon hiding behind the entrance rock. 'You'll have to tell him, you know. He has to be able to deal with it.' Then she added, with uncustomary ferocity, 'He has to be good enough.'

'I know,' I said.

'That's just it, Med – I don't think you do. I don't think you really know what that means. If you have to contort yourself like your snakes to get him to really see you, if you have to chop parts of yourself off, or hide your heart and mind – your entire self – to attract him, then you will live your life like a pauper in a queen's body.'

'But, Stheno, why would he ever like me?'

'You're worth dying for, Medusa. You're wonderful. You're the greatest joy in my life.'

'Stheno—'

125

'I want a man to treat you as if his happiness had found a home.'

'I'm not that special!'

'Never let me hear you say that again. Everyone deserves to be loved. People have never been nice enough to you, Med. Ever. They've been jealous and greedy, and then cruel and judgemental, and every time, you've believed what they had to say about you. So I don't want you to have your heart broken over the first bidder.'

'Who says he'll break my heart?'

'Just because one man is being nice now, doesn't mean he always will be.'

'So what do you want me to do, Stheno? Never try something sweet, just because it might go sour in the years to come? How is that a way to live?'

She stood up and moved towards the open air. 'If these wings were taken off me now, I'd hate it. I wouldn't feel like me. So I wouldn't hide them for any man. A man who truly loved you, would also love those snakes.'

'I know you want to protect me,' I said. 'But I have to make my own decisions now. I'm not a little girl.'

126

Stheno began to rise from the ground and started hovering round me in circles. 'But a little girl is somewhere still inside you. I see her. And I know she wants to be seen.'

'No.'

'You think that when you grow up, you shed old selves as your snakes their skins, discarded and forgotten forever? No. There are days of my childhood that feel like yesterday. I know you carry your pain. I know you're scared of your snakes.'

'Stheno. Look at my head. My childhood could belong to someone else!'

She lifted herself higher into the sky, her arms folded. 'We're all changed, Medusa, but I'm still your sister. And I want you to take care of yourself before this goes too far. If you trust him, then tell him about the snakes.'

'You're forgetting something. Remember what Athena said – Woe betide any man fool enough to look upon you!'

Stheno shrugged. 'Well, that's a risk he'll just have to take. Sometimes it pays to be a fool.'

I felt miserable. 'Promise you won't tell Euryale. Promise you won't tell?'

But by now, my beloved sister had opened her arms wide, and was beating her wings hard against the air, rising up and up above the caves, off into the blue.

For all my protestations that the old me was dead and that I was changed, the conversation with Stheno echoed inside me long after she'd flown away. I think I'd protested so much because I knew she was telling a truth.

I did want to be seen. I did want love – on my terms, as the person I truly was, snakes and all. And she had also reminded me that it was not weak to admit wanting such a thing. If that's what you wanted, it was perfectly natural. No woman is an island – unless she's been forced there by a bunch of strangers.

I resolved that when I next saw Perseus I would tell him the part of my story that I'd been most scared to share, even more than what had happened with Poseidon in the temple.

I would tell him how Athena had changed me, how these snakes that writhed and wriggled above my hairline were no temporary state of affairs, but were intrinsic to my soul, to my spirit, my wakened days and slumbering nights. I would tell him how my real name barely began to touch who I was. And I'd promised, hadn't I? I trusted him. I'd made the first promise I truly wanted to keep.

And when I told him everything, then he would see.

Chapter Eleven

Later that day, Perseus and I were sitting in our normal places, either side of the entrance rock. The afternoon had taken on a calm quality, the sea beyond the cliff as glassy as a mirror, reflecting back nothing but the echo of a cloudless sky.

'Do you like living in a cave?' Perseus asked suddenly.

I considered the question. At night, the cave could be damp, but it was roomy, and the rocks made beautiful patterns when the firelight danced on them. But I did miss my old house, and I said as much.

'You could build a house here, with that view,' he said. 'Or I could build one.'

I laughed. 'Have you ever built a house?'

'No, but there's a first time for everything. Just

imagine – a nice, cool, whitewashed house, with dividing rooms, and a well in the garden, and a strong roof. You could plant fruit trees. Herb bushes.'

'But what would you do once you'd built the house?' I asked. 'Would you stay in it?'

'If you'd let me. I could be your … lodger.'

'Wouldn't you miss your mum?'

'She could live here too.'

I had to laugh again. Perseus wanted me and his mother to exist in the same sphere, but there was more than an ocean dividing us. It was unlikely Danaë would want a daughter-in-law with snakes for hair, however similar our treatment had been at the hands of powerful gods. Perseus wanted things neat, organised, controllable, and I was the opposite of all of that.

I remembered Stheno's urging – to accept my true self, to expect Perseus to do the same.

'All right,' I said. 'Your mother's welcome. I charge low rent.' He didn't laugh. 'Perseus? I was only joking.'

'No, I know. I'm sorry. It's just … talking about her, it's reminding me. I haven't seen her for so long. I don't know what Polydectes might have done to her. And if I come back empty-handed, it's pain of death.'

'Empty-handed?'

He sighed. 'You know that mission I'm on?'

'Yes?'

'I never wanted it. Polydectes sent me out of the palace so he could get at my mum. I'm sailing, getting lost, sitting on rocks, when she could be his wife by now. She could even be dead.'

Perseus's voice was shaking. I wanted more than anything to go round the rock and take him in my arms, but I was still so fearful. I recalled again Stheno's insistence that Perseus had to know my true self in order for me to trust his love. But how to find the words to tell him? How to start that conversation?

'What is your mission, exactly?' I said gently, daring myself to creep nearer to his side of the rock.

'I have to save my mother,' said Perseus. To my utter surprise, he began to weep.

'Oh, Perseus. You will. I promise—'

'You don't understand,' he said. 'No one understands.'

'I will help you, Perseus. I promise. What do you have to do to save your mum?'

I edged even nearer, so that half of me was round his side, his back still turned to me.

Perseus was quiet for a moment. He hunched his shoulders and I watched the fine hairs on the nape of his neck. He took a deep, shuddering breath.

'My mission,' he said, 'is to cut off the head of the Medusa.'

We all have moments in our life when we look back and wonder whether we did the right thing. Whether if we'd said or done something different, a better outcome might have prevailed. I have thought about those moments after Perseus spoke that sentence nearly every day of my life. How afterwards, the unravelling began, how there seemed to be nothing we could do to stop it.

I can't remember exactly the order in which it all happened, but I do remember recoiling behind the safety of the rock, and pressing against it, as if to find some support in that natural structure that I could not find in myself. My breathing was very shallow, little choking sobs at the top of my throat, as if Athena had put her own hands around my windpipe and was squeezing tight. My blood seemed to have rushed to the lower half of my body; I felt light-headed, airy, my snakes close to evaporation, and yet as if my feet were made of clay.

The Medusa. What did he mean, the Medusa?

My name was Medusa, and I was a girl. Perseus had made me sound like a mythical beast. I didn't want to be a myth. I wanted to be me. To think you were going to step round the rock and reveal yourself, I thought.

'Merina?' Perseus said. His voice was very far away, as if he were talking from the other end of a tunnel.

I couldn't reply. I couldn't think in order.

In that moment, I did not feel in danger: I remember that. I thought I was safe, because Perseus still didn't know about my snakes.

'Yes?' I replied, my voice strange, constricted.

'Are you all right?' he said. 'I didn't mean to scare you, talking about the Medusa.'

In another set of circumstances, I could have laughed; the irony was so rich I could taste its marrow. 'What's ... the Medusa?' I managed to say.

My next thought was: Does Perseus know? Is this a game? Any minute now, is he going to come round to this side of the rock?

'You haven't heard of her?' he said.

'Been on this island four years, Perseus,' I wheezed. 'Haven't caught up.'

'Yeah, I guess news doesn't travel this far. The Medusa is a monster. She's hideous. Her skin's filthy. She eats lizards for breakfast.'

'She eats what for breakfast?'

'Lizards.'

'That's ridiculous,' I said.

'It's true! They say she's got a head of snakes. She's repulsive.'

Daphne, Callisto, Artemis, Echo and the other serpents on my scalp rose up and started writhing in anger. I clamped my arms across them, and backed away even further into my cave.

'Do you know anyone who's seen her?' I shouted to him.

'No one's seen her,' he shouted back.

'So how do you know she's so repulsive?'

'Everyone says it, Merina. And I just mentioned the head of snakes – isn't that repulsive enough?'

136

'But if no one's seen her, how do you know she's even real?'

'That's exactly why Polydectes sent me to find her, because he doesn't ever want me to come back,' said Perseus, his voice rising and rising in anger. 'That's why I have to find it, chop its head off, and go home.'

'You're not making sense, Perseus. How can you chop the head off something that isn't real?'

'Zeus, Merina, I don't know! That's why I'm so depressed. I'll never get home. I just have to keep believing in the monster. And one day I'll find it, and chop its head off.'

I leaned against the wall of my cave, my heart thumping. My head, still firmly attached to my neck, was reeling. I fell to my knees and crouched on all fours.

I was famous. I'd had no idea. My name was known as far as Oceanus to Perseus's city of Seriphos. How, how had this happened? Alekto and Leodes, their wayward tongues? Travelling pilgrims passing by our village, asking questions as to why that house on the hill stood empty? Who used to live there? Well, you'll never guess …

No, I thought. No mortal word would travel that far.

It had to be Athena.

Athena is a bitch.

'Do you … really think you could chop its head off?' I asked him. 'If you were to meet it?'

I couldn't believe I was having this conversation.

'If it meant saving my mother,' said Perseus, 'then yes.'

I slid on to the gravel of the cave floor and lay on my side. Of course, of course this had all been too much to hope for. I'd always known that inside new things grow the seeds of loss, but I hadn't expected my loss to be quite so immediate. I hadn't known how bad the pain would be when hope just falls away.

'Perseus,' I said, the tears coming, the words falling out of my mouth before I could really stop them. 'My whole life, the only man I ever wanted to look at me was you.'

'What are you talking about? You sound strange. Are you all right? Merina—'

'Be quiet, Perseus. I'm telling you a story.'

I sat back up, and walked towards the entrance

rock, stopping before it and not leaving my side of the cave. 'Sometimes,' I said, 'life just seems like a series of endless questions that you really don't want to answer. And you can live like that, for a while. For a while you can pretend you're deaf to the voice inside you. You can pretend to be someone you're not. You can pretend that the thoughts you're having, or the way you're feeling, aren't really true.'

'Merina, what are you talking about?'

'But it can't last. My sisters knew it. And you realised it, in the court of Polydectes. And now I know it too.'

And it's true: there's only so long you can wear the mask before the skin beneath it starts to curdle. Before you contort into a half-self. And you can't go back. Time doesn't work like that.

'I'm not Merina,' I said, and a lightness sang through me. I heard a howl of despair out in the middle of the ocean, and I knew it was Poseidon, furious that I would not be cowed. I felt as if my body were at one with the water again, as if Athena had transformed me into a dolphin. I closed my eyes and saw a starfish, its hand outstretched in a greeting of old welcome. But when I reached to grab it, my palm found only air.

'I'm not Merina,' I said again. 'And I never have been.'

'You're not Merina?' Perseus repeated, and I heard the edge of panic in his voice.

'You kept your promise, Perseus,' I said. 'And now I must keep mine.'

'I don't understand …'

'I'm the girl you're looking for,' I said.

'I knew that, the moment we first talked—'

'No, Perseus. I'm what you're looking for. I'm the Medusa.'

There was a silence. 'What?' he said.

'Perseus, I'm Medusa. Your monster is me.'

Chapter Twelve

There came a longer silence; the longest of my life. For the first time in four years, I'd spoken my real name out loud. For the first time ever, I'd told someone about what had happened to me – not just in Athena's temple, but all of it – my life so far, with all its pains and beauties. It was one of the hardest things I'd ever done, and even then I knew I wasn't finished, that my story had only just begun. My name was on the air, and I wasn't afraid of it any more. Stheno was right: it did feel good.

The sky beyond the cave was a bright, clear blue, and I could hear the waves below us, the endless music of the sea – my sea, not the sea that Poseidon thought he owned. I felt the soles of my feet rooted on to the warm ground. I felt my snakes, light and calm. I waited for Perseus to speak. I longed for him to say something: it was his turn.

Minutes passed. I could hear him breathing heavily on the other side of the rock. Still he would not speak.

'Perseus?' I said. 'Are you ever going to say something?'

'You ... I ... you can't be the Medusa,' he whispered, and even that quietly I could hear the crack in his voice.

'I'm Medusa,' I said.

'No,' he replied.

'How can you not believe me,' I said, 'when I've bound us in the truth? Can't you taste it? Tell me you can taste it.'

'Yes,' said Perseus, his voice heavy, 'I can taste it.'

'So you believe me about Poseidon, and Athena?'

'I do,' he said, sounding hoarse and scared. How could he be scared, when we had held each other's hands so tight? 'But you can't be her,' he went on, feverish. 'You can't be her.'

'I can be, and I am.'

'My mother needs—' he began.

'Your mother is just like me,' I said.

'Don't talk about my mother! My mother isn't a

monster,' he cried, and once these words were out, his voice completely broke. I felt my belief in him slip like a fish through a poorly knotted net. I said nothing. I was not going to justify myself again. I pushed away the little nub of fear that was growing in my gut. I felt Echo and Artemis begin to stir in agitation. I hushed them, keeping my eye on the horizon, keeping the warmth in the soles of my feet – and then I heard Perseus running away from the entrance rock, his footsteps fading to a different quality of silence. I was alone, just my snakes and me.

What did I feel in that moment? Stheno had told me to test Perseus, but I hadn't realised I'd been testing myself too. But while I was holding a bud of self-knowledge, it was beginning to look as if Perseus had failed. He was the one who was falling apart. He could not hold these realities together like I could – and I felt sorrow, and anger, and some odd element of relief: At least I know him now, I thought grimly. He came here for the promise of a severed head.

I wasn't standing in the dark any more. Perseus had come, not in search of love or friendship, no young man's island-hopping odyssey. Instead, a bloodstained destiny and a desire to protect his mother had put him to wandering the waters. And now he was running back to his boat, broken apart, confused.

Yet still I hoped. I didn't want to lose him, even though he was losing himself. I imagined King Polydectes setting Perseus off towards the infinite horizon, assuming he'd never see his young enemy again. The perfect wedding gift, given by the king to himself! I pictured Perseus at Seriphos harbour, barely given a chance to say goodbye to his mother. And Danaë, embracing her son in silence, knowing that words would not be enough to protect her from the king's advances. I saw that giant sword at her son's side, shining from its hilt; Perseus, walking up the gangplank; Driana, empty-handed on the harbour, turning away in tears.

I was exhausted. Knowing I was alone, I walked around the entrance arch, towards the edge of the cliff, expecting to see Perseus unfurl his sails and pull up anchor, but I saw nothing but the water. Part of me wanted to go down to the shore and make him see me in my snakely glory. Another part of me didn't. I didn't want to chase someone who'd already

144

fled. I had my snakes and I had my dignity, and I realised, for the first time, that I could not tell the difference.

The sun was setting: my sisters would be home soon. I spent the gathering dusk walking the tops of the cliffs, looking out to the fading horizon. To think that people in far-off lands should talk of my head as a trophy to be dragged home! It felt, dare I say it, almost familiar.

I didn't know what Perseus was going to do next; that was the worst of it. And what would be worse – him setting sail and leaving me forever, or coming to face me, his sword aloft? Before now, a different version of me might have welcomed my own murder – an end, at least, to any more scrutiny and punishment, of feeling uncomfortable in my own skin. Death would be an escape. Perseus would get his mother back, and I would get peace. The gods might finally be satisfied.

But I didn't want my death; I hadn't come this far to die. Deep, deep in my heart, all I wanted was for Perseus to do what Stheno had said: to see me for who I was – not a myth, not a monster, but an eighteen-year-old girl who cooked a mean octopus

145

stew and loved her dog. I wanted Perseus not to be scared to love me. I tried to banish Athena's warning from my mind. If Perseus loved me, then I might learn to love myself too, and that was what Athena feared.

But Perseus didn't come to my cave that night. Neither did he leave the island. I watched the promontory, long after our evening fire had sputtered out and Stheno, Euryale and Argentus were fast asleep. I held a vigil, my torch aloft, standing on the edge of the cliff. There was no movement below: I was a sentinel with nothing to guard.

The next morning, I slept in late, and woke refreshed. I'd slept strangely well: no dreams, just heavy oblivion, sheer exhaustion. When I opened my eyes, the sun outside the mouth of the cave was very high and my sisters were nowhere to be seen. They'd probably noticed how I'd been distracted in my own thoughts the night before, and wanted to let me be. I knew that Stheno had not mentioned Perseus to Euryale, because Euryale would have blown like a fury. My secret was safe for now, but something in my gut told me it would not be so for much longer.

I was right, of course. You should always listen to your gut.

I was washing my face when I heard the clanking of armour. When I went to look, Perseus was making his uneven way up the cliff. He was wearing his helmet and his shield, his sword and his sandals. He was coming back to me, kitted out for war. Is that it? I thought. Is love just easier when one of you no longer exists? Is it easier to keep a fantasy than a reality dressed to kill you?

Unseen, from behind a rock, my pulse pounding hard in my veins, my snakes rigid, I watched Perseus as he wended across the top of the cliff. His walk became more purposeful, but his shining head was cast down; he did not want to see this day, for all that he had made it.

I was paralysed: to run to him, or run away? But before I could make that decision, suddenly Perseus stopped, hurling down the sword and shield, falling to his knees. He raised his hands to his face, and I couldn't see whether he was making an offering to the gods or wiping away tears. I will never know which. Perseus was positioned from me as he always was: too far away.

147

I could have run then, I suppose – over the terrain, down a hidden path, finding another cove to hide in, swimming away until my sisters spotted me and carried me to safety. But I realised, watching him slowly pick up his sword again and carry that shield along the cliff, that I wasn't prepared to run any more. I'd been running from myself nearly my whole life. I had no idea what was going to happen, but I trusted that what was going to happen was right. The gods had bound us together now, and in a twisted logic, it was something I wanted. Now was the time for resolution. True knowledge of myself. No fear.

By now, Perseus was coming down the direct path towards my entrance arch, holding that moonlike shield in front of himself. Orado was barking and bounding behind him, as if agitated by his master's decisions.

All I could think of in that moment was Athena's warning: Woe betide any man fool enough to look upon you now! Whatever the goddess had meant by that, I didn't want to hurt Perseus. I thought of his mother. I didn't want to be the reason for someone else's pain. And so I made my decision, and ran back into my cave.

'Perseus,' I called to him. 'Just go home. Get out of here. Please.'

He didn't stop: I could hear him coming.

Then silence: I knew he was outside the entrance arch. I heard a light clank of his sword as it brushed against the shield.

'Friends don't lie to each other,' Perseus said. His voice was unlike I'd ever heard it: odd, colourless. He didn't sound like a hero. He didn't sound like a friend.

'I never lied,' I said. 'I told you the truth. Every last bit. You're the only person I've ever told. And I think the problem is, you know I'm telling the truth.'

At this, his footsteps started up again, and to my horror I realised that Perseus was coming round the entrance arch, towards my cave.

'Perseus, go away!' I said. 'I don't think it's safe. For either of us.'

My snakes became agitated, coiling and uncoiling, undulating wildly, hissing loudly and snapping at each other, their fangs fully bared.

'I can hear her snakes!' he cried, as if I wasn't

even there. 'Oh, gods, oh, gods – it's true!'

'Perseus, please,' I said. 'I'm not a monster. My snakes aren't bad. This one's called Callisto, this one's Daphne—'

'I don't care what they're called!'

'Perseus,' I said. My voice was hard as rock. 'Hurting me isn't going to save your mother.'

'I told you not to talk about my mother,' he said, and I could hear him coming nearer. 'I trusted you.'

'And I trusted you. And look who's holding a sword!'

'To think I told you all those things about her, about me—'

'And I was grateful for it, Perseus. You're the first person I've spoken to like that my whole life. I don't know what's going to happen here, but I fear it won't be good. You have to go. I've asked you – now I'm telling you. Please, walk away. Don't come any nearer.'

But Perseus ignored me, moving even deeper into my cave, dragging his sword in the gravel. I heard him stumble on the shield and swear under his breath. I backed away even further, and still he followed.

'Perseus!' I yelled. 'Put that sword away!'

'I can't leave here without you,' he said.

'Yes, you can.'

'Show yourself!'

I stayed hiding in the shadows. 'I don't want to go, Perseus. This is my home now. You're the one who can leave. Athena cursed me, not you.'

'You think I want this?' he said.

'Maybe you do?' I retorted. 'No one's stopping you getting back on your boat.'

'My mother—'

'Athena forced this head of snakes on me, just like Poseidon forced himself on me. Just like Polydectes forced himself on your mother. Perseus, open your eyes. I just want to live. I just want to be me.'

'I told you not to talk about her—'

Something snapped inside me. 'I'll talk about her all I want,' I said. 'And if you think I won't defend myself, then the trials of your mother have taught you nothing.'

My snakes began to hiss even louder, straining to their very tips, as if they wanted to fly off my head and wrap themselves around his.

151

'The sounds of a monster,' said Perseus. 'And the speech of one too. Oh, Hades,' he said. He sounded like he was going to cry.

It might have gone differently if I'd kept quiet about Perseus's mother. By summoning Danaë in an appeal to Perseus's mercy, he forgot my pain and thought only of his. He took another step forward into the semi-darkness. With a huge effort, he lifted the sword to his side, and death vibrated in the air. 'Come out from where you're hiding,' he said. 'Don't make me come to you.'

'You don't even know how to use that sword,' I replied, my panic rising. Artemis was practically shedding her own skin in an attempt to escape off the top of my head. 'I've seen you try to carry it.'

'I do know how to use it.'

'Perseus – you know the real me,' I said, my breath trapped in the top of my chest. 'The girl you've been talking to these past days. You said I was the only girl you could talk to—'

'Shut up, Merina! I mean, Medusa. Shut up!'

I could hear his fear. 'Perseus,' I begged. 'We like each other. We could shine together—'

'I don't want to shine with you. You knew this

152

could never be, but you strung me along. You could kill me!'

'What? How could I kill you? Leave, Perseus. I've asked, I've ordered, and now I'm begging you. Leave.'

But I heard Perseus moving even closer. 'You know I can't,' he said flatly. 'I told you my story, why I was sent away. Why I'm here.'

'You'd never do this to me,' I cried. 'I know you never would.'

From the side of the shield, Perseus lifted the sword again, the blade swinging upwards through the air. 'No, Medusa,' he said. 'I won't leave you behind.'

He had found the very back of the cave, where I was hiding. The tip of his sword nicked my arm, slicing open my skin. It was a lightning bolt to the blood, and it woke something in me. Perseus was covering himself with the shield and he was coming for me. He wanted this over.

My foot kicked out and struck the edge of his shield. I'd underestimated my strength, and Perseus staggered back. The shield rolled to the side, a grounded moon, and he was left exposed. And for the first time in four years, so was I. My snakes extended themselves into an unholy halo, all scales and fangs, a multicoloured assertion of serpentine power.

Despite his fall backwards, Perseus was still holding his sword in one hand, his free arm across his face. He got to his feet and advanced, still not looking at me, waving the blade all over the place. Watching him like this, I'd had enough. I rushed forward and grabbed the tip of the sword with both my hands, and Perseus gasped in shock. We tussled over it – I could have lost my fingers – but all I wanted was to cast it to one side, to get Perseus out of my cave and back on his boat towards his mother.

'Stop this,' I said, fighting back tears. 'All you need to do is leave.'

'No,' he said. 'I won't.'

'Are you crazy? Are you really that crazy?'

Because Perseus wouldn't look at me, his balance wasn't good. Nevertheless, he was strong, and he tugged back hard, slicing the sword out of my grasp. He swung it sideways, his free arm still over his eyes, and brought it round towards my neck.

I don't know what possessed me to do what I did

next. I ducked and came back hard, elbowing Perseus's blade out of the way. Echo, of all my snakes, was the one to lash out and nip him on the shoulder. With a cry, Perseus saw his shining sword fly from his hand, and he turned, his face bared to mine, girl to boy: eye to eye. He looked up towards my snakes, his expression all amazement.

'Medusa,' he whispered.

And then the strangest thing of all happened. As Perseus stared at me, his jaw dropped open like a trap door, his eyes frozen in petrified astonishment. His mouth turned into an O, and his skin went pale as if the gods had made a straw for his veins and sucked.

'Perseus!' I screamed. 'Perseus, what's happening?'

Too late for him to tell me: my name would be the last word he uttered. He was disappearing before my eyes, his own irises turning milky grey. His pupils vanished, his flesh turned stony, his arms stiff.

We were standing so close that I could hear the symphony of his skin cracking to stone, and I swear I heard a far-off scream that might have been his mother's. I held him, I shook him, I touched him everywhere, trying to bring life back to his limbs, but there was nothing. His feet were like effigies beneath his body, now a tomb, Perseus as his own lapidary image. And then I remembered Athena's warning: Woe betide any man fool enough to look upon you now.

I touched the hardened nub of Perseus's elbow, his fists of frozen fingers. Orado howled at his side as I stared in horror. My friend, my dream, a boy; dead and gone.

Chapter Thirteen

Some people think that we're born with our destiny mapped in our blood. But mapped by whom? By the gods? By fate, a mysterious mix of birth and starlight? We were all planned out, we just didn't know it. We tread a fully formed path, and those who stray from it will crash and die. Then there are others who believe we're born blank. Clean as spring water, we become the creators of our own hurricanes.

I think it's both. I had a map, I had a star, but I also made some hurricanes. I'm telling you this because I need you to understand what happened when Perseus turned up on my island. I made a choice, but also that choice was beyond me, waiting for its making.

I knew that Perseus and I couldn't stay either side of that arch forever. I think part of me knew it from the moment I saw him down on his boat. Stheno knew it. Even before he discovered who I was, Perseus knew it too. We both knew that time would have its way with us. But such perspicacity will not save you from the surprise when it actually does.

Did I kick that shield so he would see me, and never mind the consequence? Or did I do it to push his swinging sword away? The poets are divided. But still: I asked Perseus, again and again, not to come into the cave. I begged him to leave. And did he listen? No.

Who knows what would have happened if he'd obeyed me. If he'd sailed off, maybe he'd have found some real monsters to kill, to make his own myth – as I have here, my story finally made mine. Perseus the Brave, Perseus the King: it sounds familiar. Maybe he would have saved a maiden and married her? Maybe, in another universe, that's exactly what he did.

Not in my universe, however. In my universe, I left him on the edge of a cliff. I have to tell you something else too: I saw my face in that shield of his, and I looked good.

Perseus swung at me for a story, and it wasn't the

one I've told you here. You should be careful who tells your story. For so long, I had no choice but to listen to the noise. But I knew my time would come. I knew that one day I'd be able to tell you this.

Some days, I still can't believe how I watched Perseus's soft flesh harden to permanent rock, and left it to be weathered by the wind and rain, bleached by the sun and stained by the gulls for eternity. It seems like something that happened to a different person. Since then, I've come so far. He taught me, without realising.

After he turned to stone, I carried him out of the cave to inspect him in brighter light, and left him lying sideways in the grass, seeing as he was no longer a threat. Orado was still howling, licking the stone of Perseus's foot. My sisters, landing nearby, couldn't believe their eyes. I explained what had happened. Euryale was too fascinated by Perseus's metamorphosis to even be angry with me that I'd kept such a dangerous secret.

'And ... he just looked at you and turned to stone?' she said.

'Exactly that.'

She beamed. 'You're a powerful woman, Medusa. I'm in awe of you.' She looked over at Perseus's statue. 'We'll have to break him up,' she said, her hands on her hips, her wings half open, pacing round Perseus's inert form. 'We have to bury the evidence.'

'We can't do that,' I said. 'We have to honour his body.'

Euryale scoffed, but I was adamant. 'We have to honour what happened here, Euryale. We have to honour what I am. I'm not scared of Athena any more. She's shown me what I am, and I'm still here.'

Orado snuffled at the statue, as if the clue to his master's stasis was buried in the grass. He reached his front paws on to Perseus's kneecaps, barking with all his might for a resurrection. 'I'm sorry, Orado,' I said. The dog looked at me, the dark, wet beads of his eyes not comprehending where his master had gone, and nor could I tell him.

'Don't apologise,' said Euryale. 'You were defending yourself. But who's going to believe that, with you looking like you do, and him being the son of Zeus?'

'Perseus came here of his own accord, Medusa,' said Stheno. 'You talked with him. You shared your time with him and listened to him. You told him your name and he told you that you were a monster.'

'But he believed me, Stheno.'

'He did: but when you warned him to keep away, he didn't listen. You had no idea Athena had given you this power. I believe that the gods, however fickle, will see all that.'

'Well,' said Euryale, exhaling heavily. 'Only time will tell.'

This power.

You're a powerful woman, Medusa.

My sisters' words ran through my head. I'd been scared of other people's power my whole life, never mind my own. I gazed down at Perseus's face – those carved cheekbones, sharp as a cuttlefish, the smooth jaw, the frozen furrow between his brows, the round O of his mouth. Maybe if I kissed it, I could bring him back to life? I knelt down and placed my mouth on his: warm lips on cold stone. Nothing. This wasn't a fairytale. I wondered if I even wanted him to be resurrected. Orado was licking the hard planes of Perseus's shins and calves with the tenderness of a mother cat to her half-drowned kitten.

'Medusa,' said Stheno. 'You need to say goodbye.'

I walked around the cliff top, yanking up bunches of love-in-a-mist, forget-me-nots, seagrass and wild roses. My sisters pulled him to his feet, set him upright, looking out to sea. As best I could, I twined the stems into a wreath, and when it was finished, I placed it on Perseus's head as if it were a crown. The wind dropped, and the gulls fell quieter in their mewling. Above us, the sun beat upon our heads like the eye of a god, seeking to light the cracks inside us.

Perseus had pretended to be a warrior, a man capable of killing. But it was I who had taken that step. I was a girl, but I was also a Gorgon – which side of myself was the true one? Was I going to have to pick, or was it already a permanent kind of blend? There was nothing good about killing someone. If you do that to a person, you carry it inside yourself for the rest of your life, a prison sentence of its very own kind. Years later, Euryale would still talk about what I did to Perseus as being justified. Whenever she said this, a raven wing would beat upon my heart. As your life unfurls, what makes you so sure

162

your reasons are the right ones? You don't ever know for sure. You're simply trying to survive.

As the years passed, however, I would remember the feel of that sword in my skin more than I ever remembered Perseus. Once he raised that sword against my flesh, one of us was not going to get out of that cave alive. When Perseus came at me, I must have realised something: I was not going to let him destroy me for who I was, or who he thought I was, for his own ends. It was simply unacceptable.

'Perseus, son of Danaë,' I said now, addressing the statue. I thought he would like his mother mentioned. 'You're in Elysium now, I'm sure.'

'I think we should go,' said Euryale. 'If you don't want to break him up, then fine, but I think it's a bad idea to leave him out here. You're making a memorial that could incriminate you. Let's put him back inside the cave.'

'No,' I said. 'He stays on the cliff.'

'Medusa …' Euryale began, but Stheno silenced her with a glance.

'Do you think we'll ever come back?' I asked. 'To remember what happened?'

'Perhaps,' said Stheno, but she looked doubtful.

'Are we always going to be on the run?' I said.

Stheno took me in her arms and held me tight. 'No. From this day on, there's no more running away.'

That said, it was Stheno's idea to take Perseus's boat. We didn't want the bad memories of this island. And to take the boat made sense, she said, because we didn't know how far we were to go, and my sisters could not carry me forever. And the boat would only rot in the cove, attracting barnacles to its hull. Here was a little wooden reef of grief that we could rescue into happiness.

We took Orado, of course, alongside Argentus. At first, Orado was reluctant, giving out little yips of pain as he realised he was being removed from his position at the statue's feet. But how would he survive, with no one to feed him, trying to snap at seagulls, no company to keep? It felt like I was stealing him from Perseus, but I was growing accustomed to this new sensation of uncomfortable compromises, of living in the grey areas of life, rather than the starker strips of black and white I'd believed in as a child.

164

We threw the sword and the shield and the helmet into the sea, watching them submerge, to rust and grow as homes for creatures we would never see.

I hadn't been on a boat in over four years, but as soon as I stepped on deck, memories came back to me, from the times before Poseidon. I remembered how to sail. I remembered how to listen to the wind, to feel it on my face, to tack this way and that as my sisters flew above my head as lookouts. I was from Oceanus. I was the sailor poet. Out on the water, between no land and on no border, I was finally home.

I couldn't wait to get the nets out.

Raising the anchor that first sunny morning, I felt a sense of courage, a thrill of power, a slither of potential. While sailing was familiar, these feelings were new to me. We set off, and now I was the traveller on the boat, and Perseus was up there, stranded sightless on the cliff. Life offers you strange mirrors.

I hadn't been in the water for so long – because I'd been scared of Poseidon. But he no longer frightened me. What Poseidon did to me that night long ago has formed only one small brick in the house of me. It is a huge house, which I've built and lived in and made beautiful, despite his worst intentions. And in fact, Poseidon didn't give me nothing – he gave me the knowledge that, whatever happened to me, I was still Medusa.

The changes he and Athena had wrought upon me had left me feeling out of my own control for years, but when Perseus had come for me in that cave with his sword, something had shifted. I was proud of who I was, and I had as much right to be alive as Perseus did. They'd all tested me; they'd all tried to see if I would break. But I was tired of men and gods and goddesses dictating the ebb and flow of my happiness, my state of mind.

I'd trusted Perseus. I had thought he was my one true hope. But it turned out my one true hope was me.

Out at sea, my snakes loved the sense of movement. They were everywhere, straining this way and that to look at the dolphins and porpoises, the curious mermaids with shells threading their hair, bobbing up from the depths to stare at me in wonder. It really is something when a mermaid is the one to stare at you in wonder – but when they did, I waved, and to my utter delight, they waved back.

I felt majestic and terrifying, and I felt how I had as a little girl – that I belonged to myself. Whatever I said or whatever I did was in perfect synthesis with my soul inside. As the serpent eats its tail, every day I died with the sun, but by morning I gave birth to myself again. And where did my sisters and I go? Not towards the lands of mist and melancholy, nor to those of blood and smoke. I'd had enough of all of that, and nor did I wish to be one of those souls who wandered the world in search of something always out of reach. We stayed on the waters, and sailed.

Once upon a time I would have thought we looked like freaks – my sisters high in the sky, their wingspans wide; me down on the deck, snakes streaming like ribbons; the dogs either side of the prow, their fur so gold and silver in the sun. But now I know that we looked glorious.

In the early years after we left the island, sometimes I'd remember Perseus and I'd dream badly, waking with my mind full of Danaë and Driana wondering where their beloved boy had gone. Had Danaë been forced to marry Polydectes, or had she managed to escape such a fate? I hoped she had. I thought I could write to them. I could even visit Seriphos – maybe they would understand? But I couldn't risk it. A mother's grief would see the monster in me, not the girl who'd handed over her trust to a boy who didn't know what to do with it.

I did not want Perseus's end to be an extinction of my hopes of love. I worried, after what had happened on my island, that love only worked when you couldn't truly see the other. Was love only perfect when one of you was hiding behind a shield or a rock, or when one of you was dead, unable to answer back? We'd made each other in our own images – but in our case, Perseus hadn't bargained on a head of snakes, just as I hadn't bargained on a swinging sword. I knew now that we could never have been together, because he was unable to accept me for who I was. Stheno was right that I should tell Perseus, because in the end, he saved me from a lifetime of assuming that romance would rescue me. Did he love me? How can you love someone and want to chop off their head? Call me naive, but that's a strange kind of love. Perseus was lonely. He was drawn to me, as I

168

was to him. But in the final reckoning, something else louder than love spoke to him that day.

If I do fall for someone, and tell them the truth of my power, the agony will be mine when he decides to leave. For how can I explain to a man that I truly want him to see me, but that he will pay for such a pleasure with his life? To kiss him will be to kill him, and I couldn't trust that he would listen to my warning. Perseus had not listened. He thought he knew what he was doing. Maybe there is a man out there who will be able to keep a comfortable distance. Only the gods know that.

So now we sail on, looping the world on our stolen boat. Very occasionally, we drop anchor by a seashore, but I never go on land. Not because I'm afraid to be seen, but because I do not wish to have more unnecessary stone men on my hands. I live on the outside, in the blue depths which edge our cities, plains and beaches. This is a life sentence of its own kind – never to get close to a person, for fear that if a lover so much as laid a glance in my direction, his life would be over. I could collect men like stone playing pieces, arrange them in a tableau on the deck. Euryale would like that.

I'm not lonely. Self-awareness is a great banisher of loneliness. And my sisters, the immortals, are with me. The ocean's a companion, as are the dogs – and you, of course, here, listening. I have noticed, as we travel the world, that there are more people listening. I can sense them. I know they have their questions. I feel a deep vibrating in the earth, in the skies and stars, and I want to give my answer.

And a strange thing: perhaps it's all the time I spend with my sisters, for whom time means nothing, but I feel as if I might go on forever, or at least that my myth will. I could break into a million pieces and stalk a million minds. I could drive women to feats of fame and liberty and wonder. I might live for hundreds of years to come, crossing continents and oceans, empires and cultures. Because, unlike a statue, you cannot break up a myth or wedge it on top of a cliff. A myth finds a way to remember itself. It makes a new shape, rising out of a shallow grave in glory.

You could take away my arms and legs, my body and my breasts; you could cut off my head and still not end my myth. You will not find my answer in the puzzle of a stony foot, you will not find me in my snakes. You will not find me in my deeds, nor in poems written by long-dead men. But you will find me when you need me, when the wind hears a woman's cry and fills my sails forward. And I will whisper on the water that one must never fear the raised shield, the reflection caught in an office window, or the mirror in a bathroom.

I will tell you to look into me, and you will see. Look, Medusa, girl and Gorgon. You. Me.

Acknowledgements

Thank you to Ellen Holgate for her wonderful care and guidance in the writing of this story. To the whole team at Bloomsbury for their enthusiasm and hard work in bringing this book to life. To Juliet Mushens for her spirit and invaluable support. To Sam McQueen for endless chats about the text, read-throughs and cups of tea. And to Caravaggio for his famous portrait of Medusa that was so frightening, I knew there was something else about that girl he hadn't told us, and that one day I would write it.

Reading Group Questions

1. What fuels Medusa's journey into becoming a 'monster'? What monstrous acts does she perform that are imperative to her survival? Can they be considered monstrous if she must do them in order to survive?

2. *I felt the clash of my two selves, new and old, burdened and carefree, hideous and beautiful. How was it possible to be all these things at once?* Medusa struggles with the clash of her two selves. How do these parts of her change and develop throughout the story?

3. A key theme of this story is duality of being. Medusa: victim and victor, girl and monster. Which other characters display duality?

4. What is the symbolism of the sun and the moon in this text?

5. Medusa wanted nothing more than to be free from the gaze of others to live life as she pleased. Once alone on the island, she longs for the life of a 'young woman': to fall in love; to feel the attention of a lover. What shapes these desires? What do you think creates desire?

6. How did Medusa's refusal to be controlled play into her fate?

7. *Have you ever tasted sweet danger? It's one of the best and worst delicacies, all at once. Best, because nothing – and I repeat, nothing – in life will taste as heady and particular and deceptively right, and just for you. Worst, because once you've tasted it, anything that comes after it will only be dull.* Despite having already suffered greatly, why was Medusa craving this danger? Why was she not afraid?

8. Medusa is quick to make assumptions about Perseus's character. Based on what Perseus actually

shows her, how accurate do you think these assumptions are?

9. Medusa believes she and Perseus have plenty in common. In which ways is this true, and in which ways are they different? How do their genders affect people's perception of them, and their experiences of the world?

10. Her sisters believe her snakes are a gift, while Medusa sees them as a curse. How do Medusa's feelings towards her snakes change throughout the story? What do you think about them?

11. What is the symbolism behind the snakes – why did Athena choose them? Why are no two snakes the same? Why can't Medusa control them?

12. *'When beauty's assigned you as a girl, it somehow becomes the essence of your being. It takes over everything else you might be. When you're a boy, it never dominates who you can be.'* Medusa claims she never thought about her appearance until others brought it to her attention. Do you think

we all view ourselves through the lenses of others? When did you first think about your appearance?

13. How does Medusa's view of herself change throughout the story? How does her encounter with Perseus affect the way she sees herself?

14. In myths and legends of Greek gods, what role do women play? What other retellings cast a new light on women in history? How does Jessie's retelling allow her to drive the story in new ways we haven't seen before?

15. Perseus attacks Medusa despite their emotional connection. Was their connection genuine? What drove his assault, and how did his feelings towards her change after discovering she was a Gorgon?

16. There are parallels between the lives of Medusa and Danaë. Did Perseus see this connection? Do you think Danaë would have been able to see past the Gorgon?

17. If she could have, would Medusa have gone back in time and changed anything? Do you think she should have?

18. How does Jessie Burton's version of the myth inspire you? How do you think women of all ages can connect to the story?

19. Where do myths come from? Are there any modern myths? What can we learn from them?

This book is also available as an illustrated gift edition

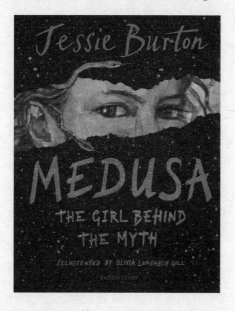

'A beautiful and profound retelling. Burton's text
and Lomenech Gill's art are a perfect match,
offering a powerfully feminist, elegiac and original
twist on this old story'
Madeline Miller

'The illustrations by Olivia Lomenech Gill are so
exquisite I would frame every single one and put
them on my wall'
Jennifer Saint

**Read Jessie Burton's outstanding debut
children's story**

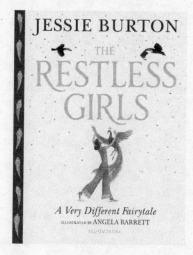

'A magical, modern fairytale … Exquisite'
Jacqueline Wilson

'A riveting feminist retelling'
Madeline Miller

'A complete revelation'
Thandie Newton

'Wild, wise, generous, ferocious'
Katherine Rundell

Read on for an extract from Jessie Burton's novel

THE
HOUSE
OF
FORTUNE

The year 1705

An Inheritance

I

At eighteen, Thea is too old to be celebrating birthdays. Rebecca Bosman turned thirty in December and never mentioned it: that is sophistication. In bed, in the dark January dawn, Thea shivers under her sheets. She can hear her aunt and Cornelia bickering down in the salon, and her father dragging away the table for breakfast on the rug. They always start Thea's birthday sitting on that rug. Relentless tradition, the fun of pretending to be adventurers, making do with the provisions they have mustered. These days it's a pitiful conceit, because none of them have left the city walls for years. Also: what's wrong with a table? They've clung on to the good one: they should use it. Adults use tables. If Rebecca Bosman had to endure a birthday breakfast, *she* would have a table.

But Thea cannot tell them any of this. Cannot bear to go downstairs and see her Aunt Nella turn away, tugging the tatty paper chains she's surely hung off the huge iced windows. Her father, staring at the threadbare rug. Cornelia, her old nursemaid, gazing forlornly at the little pufferts she's been up all night finessing. Thea has no wish to tip them into sadness, but she doesn't know how to extricate herself from this role they have put her in, their collective child. She might have become a woman today, but joy in this household is laced always with a fear of loss.

And here it comes, in the form of food, the sweet spiced waft from downstairs arriving underneath her bedroom door. The pufferts infused with rosewater, no doubt spelling Thea's name in case she should forget. Cornelia's fluffy cumin eggs to keep her prisoner, hot buttered rolls to warm her up. Delft butter, as a treat, and a thimble of sweet wine for the adults. Thea throws back the sheets, but still cannot bring herself to get up, feeling no lift of her spirits at the promise of special butter. The only thing she can hope for is that they have bought her tickets to the Schouwburg, so she can see Rebecca Bosman perform again. And afterwards, when the play is over, she can steal away to Walter, the only person who can propel her from her covers.

Soon, Thea thinks. Soon we will be together, and everything will feel right. But for now: prolonged and stale childhood.

Eventually mustering the will to put on her slippers and gown, moving slowly down the stairs in order not to be heard, Thea forces herself to be grateful. She must try not to disappoint them. Her family's over-the-top birthday cheer never used to bother her, but there is an ocean of difference between childhood and being eighteen. They are going to have to start treating her like an adult. And maybe this year, for the first birthday ever in Thea's life, someone will give her a present she really wants, and talk about her mother, give the gift of a story, or just an anecdote! Yes, we all know that today is the hardest day in the Brandt family calendar. Yes, eighteen years ago today, Marin Brandt died in this very house, giving Thea life. But who could find this day harder than me, Thea thinks as she moves across the hallway tiles – I, who have grown up motherless?

Every year, all they talk about is how much bigger Thea has grown in twelve months, how much bonnier, or cleverer, as if Thea is a brand-new person every time. As if, on every eighth day of January, which is always cold and always blue, she has come to them hatched from an egg. But Thea doesn't want to have her growth reflected back at her. She has the mirror for that. On her birthday, she wants to look into the glass and see her mother, to know who she was and why her father will never speak of her. Why almost all her questions are answered by the exchange of sombre looks and pursed lips. She hesitates, her back pressed against the wall. Perhaps even now they could be talking about Marin Brandt.

Expert eavesdropper, Thea waits in the shadows outside the salon, her breath held tight with hope.

No. They are squabbling about whether Lucas the cat will consent to wearing a birthday ruff. 'He hates it, Cornelia,' says her aunt. 'Look at his eyes. He'll vomit on the rug.'

'But it makes her laugh.'

'Not if she's eating pufferts by a pile of sick.'

Lucas, their yellow-eyed god of scraps, mewls in indignation. 'Cornflower,' Thea's father intervenes. 'Let Lucas go unclothed for breakfast. Allow him that. Maybe he can dress for dinner.'

'You two have no sense of occasion,' Cornelia retorts. 'He *likes* it.'

These familiar rhythms, these voices: Thea has known so very little else. She closes her eyes. She used to love to listen to Cornelia, her Aunt Nella, her father, to sit at their feet or to hang round their necks, being adored and petted, squeezed and teased. But these days, it is not the kind of music that interests her, it's not their necks she wants to hang around.

And this conversation about whether or not their enormous cat should wear a ruff gives Thea a fierce urge to be anywhere else. To be away from them, and start her own life, because not a single one of them knows what it is to be eighteen.

She takes a deep breath, exhales, goes in. As one, her family turn to her, and their eyes light up. Lucas trots over, dainty with his weight. The paper chains are strung along the windows, as she knew they would be. Like Thea, her family are still in their nightclothes – another Thea Birthday Tradition – and it is mortifying to see the contours of their old bodies. True enough, her Aunt Nella is clinging on fairly well at thirty-seven, but her father is forty-one, and a man of forty-one should be fully dressed before he comes to breakfast. Cornelia has such wide hips – is she not embarrassed by the way the light shines through her shift? I would be embarrassed, Thea thinks. I am never going to let my body flap about like that. Still, they cannot help it. Cornelia will always say: 'You get old, get wider hips, then die.' But Thea is going to be like Rebecca Bosman, who can fit into clothes she wore when she was Thea's age. The secret, Rebecca says, is to walk very quickly past any bakery. Cornelia would not agree.

'Happy birthday, Teapot!' Cornelia beams.

'Thank you,' Thea says, trying not to wince at the nickname. She scoops up Lucas and goes over to where they are all gathered on the rug.

'So tall!' says her father. 'When will you ever stop growing? I can't keep up.'

'Papa. I have been this height for two years.'

He takes her in his arms and gives her a long hug. 'You're perfect.'

'She's Thea,' says her aunt.

Thea meets her aunt's eyes and lets Lucas down. It's always Aunt Nella who tries to drag her father back from the brink of overpraise. Always Aunt Nella, the first to find fault.

'Let's eat,' Cornelia says. 'Lucas, no—' – for the cat, ruff-less and unencumbered, already has a piece of egg in his mouth. He skitters away to the corner, his back legs a pair of sandy pantaloons. It is common for Amsterdammers to dislike animals in their homes, fearing paw prints will mar new-scrubbed floors, droppings left in clean places, furniture massacred. But Lucas is indifferent to popular opinion. He has his private perfection and he is Thea's constant comfort.

'The greediest creature on the Herengracht,' says Aunt Nella. 'Won't catch mice, but happy to eat our breakfast.'

'Leave him,' Thea says.

'Teapot,' says Cornelia. 'Here are your birthday pufferts.' She presents them, THEA BRANDT spelled out in tiny pancakes. 'There's rosewater syrup, or if you'd like something more savoury with them—'

'No, no, this is fine. Thank you.' Thea sits down on the rug, folding her legs beneath her and popping two pufferts in quick succession into her mouth.

'Slowly!' Cornelia chides. 'Otto, a buttered roll with egg?'

'Please,' he replies. 'My knees won't take the rug. I'll sit on a chair, if no one minds.'

'You're not eighty,' says Aunt Nella, but Thea's father ignores her.

The women sit on the rug. Thea feels ridiculous and is glad no one looking in from the street can see. 'A thimble of wine for you?' Aunt Nella asks.

Thea sits up, resting her plate on her knee. 'Really?'

'You're eighteen. No longer a child. Here.' Aunt Nella hands over a small glass.

'From Madeira,' offers her father. 'They had an unaccounted barrel at the VOC, half-price.'

'Thank goodness it was,' says her aunt. 'We can't just be buying barrels of Madeira.'

Irritation flits across his face, and Aunt Nella flushes, staring down into the swirls of the rug.

'Let us make a toast,' Thea's father continues. 'To our Thea. May she always be safe—'

'—well fed,' says Cornelia.

'— and happy,' Thea adds.

'And happy,' echoes her aunt.

Thea swallows the wine, a bright hard shock glowing in her stomach to give her courage. 'What was it like,' she asks, 'the day that I was born?'

Silence on the rug, silence from the chair. Cornelia reaches for another roll and stuffs it with fluffy egg. 'Well?' Thea says. 'You were all there.'

Aunt Nella turns to Thea's father. Their eyes meet.

'You *were* there, weren't you, Papa?' Thea says. 'Or did I come into the world alone?'

'We all come into the world alone,' her aunt says. Cornelia rolls her eyes. Thea's father says nothing. It's always the same.

Thea sighs. 'You were not happy I was born.'

Her family comes alive and turns to her, aghast. 'Oh, no,' says Cornelia. 'We were so happy! You were a blessing.'

'I was the end of something,' says Thea.

Aunt Nella closes her eyes.

'You were a beginning,' her father says. 'The best beginning ever. Now: I think it's time for gifts.'

Thea knows she has been defeated, again. The easiest course of action is to eat another buttered roll and unwrap the gifts they have gathered. A box of her favourite cinnamon biscuits from Cornelia, and from her father and aunt – yes, they have been paying attention to some part of her soul at least – a pair of tickets for today's afternoon showing of *Titus*. 'Gallery seats?' she says, her heart rising. This is generous indeed. 'Oh, thank you!'

'Not every day you turn eighteen,' her father smiles.

'We can make a day of it,' Cornelia says. 'You and me.'

Thea looks at their brightened expressions. She can tell they have already planned who will accompany her – it makes sense, she supposes, for her father will have to leave soon for his clerking at the VOC, and her aunt dislikes the playhouse. 'Thank you, Cornelia,' she says, and her old nursemaid gives her hand a squeeze.

Titus is a violent play if ever there was, but Thea's favourites are the romances. Woodland idylls, island dreams, where everything is muddled before being put right. Since the age of thirteen Thea has been dragging either her aunt or Cornelia to the city playhouse. Arriving early, paying their entrance fees and the two-stuiver surcharge for standing seats, no hope of affording the dress circle, let alone a box, waiting for the place to fill with six hundred and ninety-nine other bodies. Her escapes into comedy or tragedy feel like a kind of homecoming. At the age of sixteen, after much begging and wheedling, and despite Cornelia's vehement reluctance, her family agreed she could occasionally make the five-minute walk to the playhouse on her own, as long as she came straight back home. Until meeting Walter backstage six months ago, Thea has kept her side of the bargain. But things are changing. Deceptions have been necessary. She has exaggerated the lengths of performances to steal the extra time with him. She has even fabricated play titles and show days to go backstage to find him. Her family have never doubted her. They have never checked whether this farce or that tragedy is being staged. And although at times Thea feels guilty, her and Walter's love is too important. Theirs is an unwritten romance performed in the back corridors of the Schouwburg, the words of which are indelible, inscribed as they are in the heart. Thea knows she will never give it up.

'Don't forget about this evening,' says her aunt.

Thea looks up from the pair of tickets in her hand. 'This evening?'

She sees it: the quick, shallow inhalation of breath that indicates her aunt's irritation. 'You had forgotten?' says Aunt Nella. 'The Sarragon Epiphany Ball. Thea, it's a miracle we were invited. I've been paying court to Clara Sarragon since Michaelmas to make it happen.'

Thea glances at her father's stony expression, and decides to risk it. 'You don't like those people. Why are we even going?'

'Because we have to,' Aunt Nella says, stalking towards the long, wide windows of the salon to look out across the stretch of the Heren canal.

'But why do we have to?' Thea presses.

No one answers. So Thea decides to play her last card. 'Doesn't Clara Sarragon own plantations in Surinam?'

The atmosphere in the room sharpens. Thea knows that her

father was taken to that colony and made a slave, and at the age of sixteen he was brought by her now-dead uncle to Amsterdam. She has been told just one story about that time by Cornelia, about how Amsterdam women would put songbirds in her father's hair, an image that has always made Thea feel a profound discomfort. But beyond that, a real knowledge of her father's past is hidden in a well she cannot dredge. Where her father was before that time in Surinam, or what shape his time in the colony took, Thea knows nothing. He never talks of it. It is a blank as profound as the silence around her white mother, another of the unspoken things which permeate this house like mist. Otto Brandt: he too might have hatched from an egg.

Thea is fed up with their silences. Whenever she pushes Cornelia, she receives the same response: 'I came from the orphanage,' Cornelia will say. 'And your father was taken from his first home. It is the way of things for us. This house is our harbour. It's where we stay. Where we belong.'

But what if you don't want to be in the harbour any more? Thea wonders to herself, but never dares to say out loud. What if you feel that you don't belong?

'What Clara Sarragon owns or does not own has nothing to do with you,' her aunt is saying in a hard voice. None of them look at Thea's father. 'Do not forget. Six o'clock tonight. We'll be ready in the hallway in our finery.'

'What's left of it,' says Thea.

'Precisely,' her aunt sighs.

'Go and dress, Teapot,' Cornelia says in a bright voice. 'I'll come up and help you with your hair.'

Thea glances at her father, who is now looking out of the window. Feeling a faint sheen of shame, she turns on her heel, leaving her family marooned inside the salon. As she ascends the staircase into the gloom of the upper corridor, Thea puts the Sarragon ball and her careless mention of Surinam out of her mind, and thinks about her real birthday treat. She will be happy to witness Rebecca creating magic on the stage, but behind those painted backdrops, something much more real waits. The love of Thea's life, her reason for living. No dreary party held by an Amsterdam grandee could ever ruin the promise of Walter Riebeeck.

About the Author

Jessie Burton is the author of four novels for adults, *The Muse* (2016), *The Confession* (2019), *The Miniaturist* (2014) and its sequel *The House of Fortune* (2022), and is both a *Sunday Times* no. 1 bestseller and a *New York Times* bestseller. *The Miniaturist* sold a million copies worldwide in its first year and has also been adapted for television by the BBC. Jessie is now published in forty languages. Her first children's story, *The Restless Girls*, was published by Bloomsbury in 2018.